CLAIM

FURY BROTHERS
BOOK 5

ANNA HACKETT

Claim

Published by Anna Hackett

Copyright 2024 by Anna Hackett

Cover by Hang Le Designs

Cover image by Wander Aguiar

Edits by Tanya Saari

ISBN (ebook): 978-1-923134-37-9

ISBN (paperback): 978-1-923134-38-6

ISBN (special edition paperback): 978-1-923134-39-3

WHAT READERS ARE SAYING ABOUT ANNA'S ACTION ROMANCE

The Powerbroker - Romantic Book of the Year (Ruby) winner 2022

Heart of Eon - Romantic Book of the Year (Ruby) winner 2020

Cyborg - PRISM Award Winner 2019

Unfathomed and Unmapped - Romantic Book of the Year (Ruby) finalists 2018

Unexplored – Romantic Book of the Year (Ruby) Novella Winner 2017

Return to Dark Earth – One of Library Journal's Best E-Original Books for 2015 and two-time SFR Galaxy Awards winner

At Star's End – One of Library Journal's Best E-Original Romances for 2014

The Phoenix Adventures – SFR Galaxy Award Winner for Most Fun New Series and "Why Isn't This a Movie?" Series

Beneath a Trojan Moon – SFR Galaxy Award Winner and RWAus Ella Award Winner

Hell Squad – SFR Galaxy Award for best Post-Apocalypse for Readers who don't like Post-Apocalypse

"Like Indiana Jones meets Star Wars. A treasure hunt with a steamy romance." – SFF Dragon, review of *Among Galactic Ruins*

"Action, danger, aliens, romance – yup, it's another great book from Anna Hackett!" – Book Gannet Reviews, review of *Hell Squad: Marcus*

Sign up for my VIP mailing list and get your *free box set* containing three action-packed romances.

Visit here to get started: www.annahackett.com

BELL

I turned up the collar of my jacket. A light rain was falling, and I was feeling chilled.

Scanning the street of the podunk town that lay halfway between Houston and New Orleans, I let out a sigh and crossed the road. There wasn't much to it. There were a couple of cheap motels, some retail stores that had already closed for the day, and a gas station where the Greyhound bus stopped. The lights were on in the attached diner. It looked welcoming, and I needed a coffee.

Hitching up my backpack, I headed for the door. As a habit, I tightened my grip on the strap. The bag held all my possessions. Everything I had in the world.

When you were on the run, you couldn't take very much with you.

And so much got left behind.

I hunched my shoulders and walked inside. A bell above the door jingled. An older blonde woman wearing a white apron and holding a coffee pot nodded at me.

"Take a seat, hon. I'll be with you in a minute."

With a nod, I took a seat at a table near the window. I watched a car drive past and scanned the growing shadows on the sidewalks.

There were no lurking silhouettes. No one was watching me.

Swallowing, I looked at the menu. The plastic was scarred and faded, and I ran my finger over a groove where someone had bent it once. I didn't have a lot of money left, so I couldn't splurge.

Loud voices echoed through the diner. Glancing sideways, I spotted three guys in their twenties at a booth, laughing and joking, as though they didn't have a care in the world.

They probably didn't. They probably worked, hung out, partied on the weekends. I wondered what that felt like.

An older, dark-haired guy sat a few tables away in the other direction, his head down as he read a newspaper.

The waitress appeared. "What can I get you?"

I shot her a small smile. "Coffee, please. Black. What's today's special?"

"Meatloaf. It's not fancy, but the cook has a special recipe. I promise it's hearty and filling."

And cheap. "Meatloaf, it is."

With a nod, the waitress—whose name tag said Karen—headed back toward the counter.

I drummed my fingers on the Formica table. I needed to decide where I was going. North? I could head to Memphis, or St. Louis. Or should I continue east? To New Orleans, or even Florida.

For a second, I wondered how my mom was doing back in Dallas. It'd been almost a year since I'd seen her.

It's safer this way, Bell.

But that didn't stop the pain. I missed her so much.

I'd always wanted to go to New Orleans. I tapped the table again. Then again, Florida had the beach. Who didn't like warm weather and golden sand?

The front door opened, and a young couple entered, accompanied by a gust of cold air. The man had his arm around a slim woman with red hair. She was smiling up at him.

All of a sudden, my vision blurred.

Allison.

The image of my best friend—with her wide smile, freckles, and long, red hair—was stamped in my head. I had so many images of her.

We'd been best friends since the second grade. Since the day she'd sat down beside me in class and announced that we were going to be best friends forever. And we had been. Through elementary school, middle school, and high school. Then, we'd decided to go to college together at Baylor. I'd studied business, and Allie had wanted to be a nurse.

Helping people when they need it, it's important, Bell.

She'd been the nicest person I'd ever known, with a good heart. She'd just been good and beautiful.

My hands curled around the edge of the table, and time clicked back in. I blinked and saw the redhead and her boyfriend take a seat at a table.

She wasn't Allison.

Allie was dead.

My belly revolted, tying itself in a knot. I tasted bile in my mouth, and breathed through the sensation. I dug my fingers into my thighs, pressing into the denim of my worn jeans.

"Here you go."

Karen set a mug of coffee and a plate of food down. The smell hit me, making my nausea worse. I managed a smile. "Thank you."

She eyed me. "You need anything else, hon, you let me know."

I nodded. That small bit of kindness made tears prick my eyes.

There hadn't been much kindness in my life since I'd left home.

Shaking my head, I locked it down, and picked up my fork. *Survive.* That was what was important. And I, Bellamy Sanders, was a fucking survivor.

I wouldn't let *him* win.

I ate one bite of my meatloaf, chewing slowly. I was on my third mouthful, when someone stepped up to my table.

"Hi there, sweetheart." It was one of the men from the loud trio. He had light brown hair, and a face he probably thought was handsome, but just looked ordinary. He slipped his hands into the pockets of his jeans. "You look like you could use some company. Why don't you come join us?"

I shot him a bland look. "I'd like to be alone."

"Come on now." The smile he shot me told me he thought he was charming. "I'm a nice guy." He leaned closer. "We could have some fun together."

Ugh. I hated pushy guys like this. I'd unfortunately learned that when you were a woman alone, you attracted guys like this. A lot.

"I'm fine. Thank you."

A frown formed, creasing his forehead. "Hey, I'm being friendly here."

"I just really want to eat my dinner."

"You can eat it with me and my friends." He waved at his table. "We can get to know each other."

My heartbeat picked up. He wasn't going to let it go. He was going to make a scene.

I sighed. "Look—"

A shadow fell over the table, and I lifted my head.

My heart skipped a beat.

It was the lone man from the other table. Since he'd been sitting, I'd missed an important fact. He was huge. He was tall, broad, and all muscle. The sleeves of his blue shirt were rolled up, and his arms were covered in tattoos. The ink was a mix of different designs like flowers and swirls, and cool geometric patterns.

His face wasn't exactly handsome, but I couldn't look away. He was rugged, with a nose that had been broken before, shaggy, black hair, and a black beard covering his strong jaw.

His storm-cloud eyes trained on my unwanted visitor. "She said she wasn't interested."

"Stay out of this." The younger man kept his gaze on me. "This isn't your business."

"Yeah, it is, because you're being an ass. Go."

Mr. Persistent turned to face the older man, then he froze.

I hid a smile. *Yes, that's right, you aren't the biggest guy in the room.*

"*Now,*" the tattooed giant growled.

The pest clearly weighed his options, then sniffed. "She's not worth it anyway." He sauntered back to his friends.

I kept staring at the stranger. I couldn't look away.

His head turned back to me, and storm-gray eyes met mine.

2

BEAU

The young woman looked up at me with the biggest blue eyes I'd ever seen.

"Thanks," she said.

She had a surprisingly smoky voice.

"I hate assholes like that," I told her.

She nodded. She had dyed, mousey-brown hair that was pulled back in a braid. I could tell the color wasn't natural, because it was all one color, with no variation. She had a cute face with a button nose.

"Can I buy you a coffee, as a thank you?" she asked hesitantly. She waved at the seat across from her.

"Thought you didn't want any company?"

"Not *his* company." She shook her head. "Sorry, you probably just want to finish your dinner alone. Thanks, again."

I eyed her. There was something so alone about her. I'd seen the look plenty of times before, when I'd been growing up as a kid in foster care, and now with the foster kids I trained at my gym.

"Let me get my stuff."

I'd finished my burger, so I grabbed my newspaper and coffee mug. I waved to the waitress and slipped into the seat across from the waif.

I'd clocked her when she'd first entered the diner, and initially, I'd thought she was a teenager. But now, up close, I guessed she was probably in her early twenties. Young, but she had a gritty look in her eyes.

She was no delicate flower.

My boxing career had taught me to gauge a person's grit and determination quickly. It was why I'd been so good at fighting.

My instincts told me that this woman had plenty of resilience, and she didn't give up easily.

"I'm Beau."

She hesitated. "Bell."

It probably wasn't her real name. She was clearly in trouble, or trying to outrun trouble.

"Where you headed, Bell?"

"Florida."

I nodded. "I'm on my way home to New Orleans. Had a business trip in Houston."

Some of the guys I trained in my gym had fought in a competition in Houston. I'd decided to drive instead of fly, and take my newly restored car for a spin. I'd left the boxing competition this evening, but after I'd crossed the Louisiana border, I'd decided to find a hotel for the night, and drive the rest of the way home in the morning. Maybe get off the Interstate, and take a scenic route through the wetlands.

I could have found a nice hotel—I had the money—

but I'd decided to go old school and find a motel where I could keep my car out front.

"I've always wanted to visit New Orleans." Bell toyed with her coffee mug. "It sounds great."

I laughed briefly. "Most people usually focus on the crime rate and the hurricanes."

Her lips quirked. "I think of Bourbon Street, Mardi Gras, Cajun food, the bayou."

"It has all those things. I think it's a great city."

My brothers and I did our best to help make it better. We were all successful, and tried to give back. We donated a lot of money to local charities and causes. We kept our little corner of New Orleans—a city block of the Arts/Warehouse District—crime free.

We weren't afraid to tangle with assholes who stepped onto our turf. I flexed my hand under the table. We all had our businesses and homes there, and we did what we had to do to protect it. Yes, we'd done well for five abandoned boys who'd met in foster care.

Who'd shed blood, and had each other's backs.

Older, uglier memories stirred. I let them. I never forgot where I came from.

Or who I came from.

"So, what's in Florida?"

"The beach." Bell smiled.

It lit up her face and my breath caught. Damn, she was beautiful when she smiled. I cleared my throat.

"I like the beach," she continued.

"Plenty to like—sand, warm sun, cold beers. Although there are sharks and sunburn. Once, I was on vacation with my brothers. A fin popped up in the water,

9

and I've never seen my brother Reath swim so fast. Turned out it was a dolphin."

Bell laughed, then looked startled, like she hadn't laughed very much lately. "How many brothers do you have?"

"Four."

"*Four*. Wow. I bet your place was rowdy growing up."

I lifted my chin, but didn't mention foster care. Our last foster home hadn't been pretty. Harvey Tucker had liked to beat boys in the name of discipline. Really, he'd just been a sadistic asshole.

"You have siblings?" I asked.

Her gaze dropped. "No. It was just me and my mom."

Our coffee got refilled, and I kept the conversation light. Whenever things got too personal, Bell got skittish. We talked more about New Orleans, music, movies. I wasn't much of a talker usually, but it was easy with her.

She was young and fresh, and clearly educated, despite the well-worn clothes. She should be starting her career and dating and going out with girlfriends, not doing whatever it was she was doing.

"We're closing up soon," Karen called out.

I lifted my chin. "Thanks."

Bell was biting her lip, and looking outside. The drizzle of rain had increased to a steady shower. I knew the forecast said it was going to get worse.

"You staying at the motel next door?" I glanced out the window and could just see my car. "The place isn't fancy, but it's clean."

"Um, the bus is coming through in a couple of hours."

I stiffened. The diner was closing, and it was raining. Where the hell was she going to wait?

She carefully counted out some cash and left it on the table, then gathered up her backpack. She pulled it over her shoulder.

I dropped some cash beside hers on the table and followed her outside.

Just then, there was a violent crack of thunder, and lightning filled the sky. The heavens opened and rain poured down in a torrent.

"Oh no." Bell's hair was drenched in seconds.

"Come on." I took her arm, and jogged toward the motel.

We huddled under the walkway outside my room. Our clothes were saturated, and the rain hammered down around us.

Shit. It didn't look like it was going to let up any time soon.

3

BELL

I wrapped my arms around myself. The rain poured down—drumming on the roof and rushing through the drainpipes.

My clothes were wet, my hair was wet, my bag was wet.

Beau stood beside me. At least, for once, I wasn't alone.

He shook his head, and water flew from his thick hair. I grinned. He reminded me of a wet dog.

A big, sexy tattooed one.

"I'd better go," I said.

"Where?" he demanded.

He was worried about me. I could tell he was the kind of guy who'd worry about a woman who was on her own. "You're a nice guy, Beau."

He snorted. "I'm not a nice guy. No one ever says that."

"You are. I'm good at spotting them." Actually, I was better at spotting the *not* nice guys.

He snorted again. "Did you actually look at me?" He held out one tattooed, muscular arm. "I'm the kind of guy mothers warn their daughters to avoid."

I shook my head. Beau might be big, rugged, and tattooed, but I could tell he was good to the bone. "I'm not buying it. My mother taught me to never judge a book by its cover."

"Why aren't you with your mom, instead of in this crappy town waiting for the bus?"

My stomach clenched and I looked away. "You don't have to worry about me."

He stepped closer. "But I will."

Something warm unfolded in my belly. It was nice knowing that someone was worried about me.

I reached up and touched his beard-covered jaw. "I have to go."

I took a step back...and my foot slipped on the wet concrete.

Beau moved, lightning fast. He grabbed my arm, and we slammed together.

Oh, God. He was all hard muscle, and so much heat pumped off him.

"You're so warm," I murmured.

"Are you cold?" Strong fingers curled around my arms.

I swallowed. "I've been cold for a long time."

And for a few hours, I wanted so desperately to feel warm and safe.

I pressed into his big body.

He groaned. "Damn, you smell so good."

I had one bottle of my favorite perfume—Marc

Jacobs' Daisy Ever So Fresh—that I'd allowed myself to bring when I ran. It had always been my favorite. The bottle was almost empty and I rationed it like crazy.

My hands kneaded the fabric of his shirt, and the hard muscles beneath it. I wondered if there were more tattoos under the cotton.

He leaned down, and I heard him drag in a deep breath.

Then I threw caution to the wind and leaped up.

He caught me and I wrapped my legs around his waist. I wanted to kiss him, but I'd stopped kissing over a year ago. It was too intimate.

Instead, I attacked his ear, nibbling on his earlobe. His low growl echoed around us.

"Bell... Dammit, you're too young for me."

"I'm an adult, Beau. And there are no rules about age."

"How old are you?"

"Old enough."

"Bell..."

"Fine." I scraped my teeth down his neck. His big hands clenched on my ass, and I rubbed against him. I felt the bulge of his erection and bit my lip. It was a large one.

"I'm twenty-three." Almost. I would be in one week.

"You're a baby. I'm much older than you. Too old."

I guessed he was in his late thirties. "I say you're just right." I met his gaze. "I'm old enough to know what I want."

He was quiet for a moment. "What's that?"

"To forget for a while." My voice turned to a whisper. "To not be alone."

Something flashed in his gray eyes. Like lightning in storm clouds.

"I know I want you inside me," I murmured.

He groaned again and his head moved toward mine. "I'm going to go to hell."

My fingers tightened on his shoulders. "Um, but no kissing."

I couldn't handle it if he kissed me. I'd want more, I'd want too much.

It would hurt too much when he was gone.

"Okay," he said. "What about kissing you in other places?"

I squirmed, imagining all the places this man could kiss me. "That's fine."

"I'm definitely going to hell." He spun, holding me with ease as he fumbled in his pocket. He pulled out a key and opened the motel room door.

I smiled. "I think it might be worth it."

Storm-cloud eyes met mine. "I think so, too." He carried me inside the darkened room.

It wasn't fancy. It was like a million other motel rooms across America—double bed with a colorful cover, TV, a circular, wooden table with two chairs.

He hitched me higher, and his mouth found my neck. His delicious beard scraped over my skin, and I gasped.

He set me down on my feet and backed up. He sat on the edge of the bed, then reached over and turned on the lamp. It bathed the room in a warm glow.

His wet shirt stuck to him, outlining the heavy ridges of his chest and stomach. My gaze dropped.

Oh. And the hard, intimidating bulge in his jeans.

He dangled his hands between his legs. "Take those wet clothes off, angel."

There was hot desire in his face, and need in his voice. My skin flushed hot.

I wanted to undress for him. I let my backpack slide off my shoulders. Then I unbuttoned my shirt and dropped it to the floor. It hit with a wet slap.

In my life before, I'd had lots of cute sets of underwear. It had been the thing I liked to splurge on when I had the money. I was damn glad right now that I had on a sheer, black-lace bra.

He reached out and cupped my breast. My nipples were hard points. Beau growled.

I felt that sound between my legs.

I lowered my hands and unbuttoned my jeans, then pushed them off. I stood there in just my bra and black lace thong.

I was well aware that I was slightly above average height, and a little too thin for my frame. I'd added some muscle over the last year but lost some weight. I had no super lush curves. But the way Beau looked at me made me feel beautiful.

"Come here," he growled.

4
___

BEAU

Damn, she was beautiful.

She had long, slim limbs, a flat belly, and high, firm breasts. There was toned muscle in her thighs and arms, something a man like me appreciated. Her sexy underwear just enhanced her athletic build.

She stepped closer and I caught the scent of her fruity-sweet perfume. She smelled like mangoes. I lifted a hand and ran it up her belly. I watched her suck in a breath. My hand traveled upward, and I cupped one of her breasts again.

She granted me a soft gasp and pushed into my touch. Her skin was so smooth. It reminded me that she was young.

Too fucking young for me.

But the gaze on mine—bold, and filled with honest need—was anything but young.

I couldn't push her away. I wasn't strong enough.

I pulled her closer, reached around her and

unclipped her bra. The lace slid off and hit the carpet. I reached up and toyed with one pink nipple.

She moaned.

"You like that?"

"*Yes.*"

She took another step until she was standing between my spread knees. I leaned forward and put my mouth on her nipple. I sucked hard, and her hands slid into my hair.

As I explored her, she made husky sounds. Oh yeah, I liked that. I moved my mouth across to the other breast, lapping at her skin. She couldn't stand still as I nibbled on her nipple.

I curled my hands around her slim waist. She was perfect. There was nothing fake or practiced about her.

Just pure, honest desire.

"What do you need, angel?"

"You to keep touching me." Her voice was breathy.

I slid a finger in the side of her thong, toyed with it. I smoothed my other hand around her ass cheek and squeezed. She stepped closer.

"How do you feel?" I asked.

"Hot. Naughty." She shifted on her bare feet. "Pretty damn happy that a big, delicious man like you stopped at my table in the diner."

I growled and my cock pulsed. I sucked on that sweet nipple again, pulling it deep into my mouth.

She whimpered, fingers twisting in my hair. I pushed the lace thong down, and she kicked it away.

"You're so perfect, Bell. Beautiful."

She blinked down at me.

Had no one told her that before? I slid my hands into the neat, dark curls between her legs, and she widened her stance.

"I knew you'd be soft here." I stroked her folds, and watched her bite her lip. Her hands rested on my shoulders, digging in hard. "Mmm, and you're wet for me." I teased her entrance.

"Beau... I ache."

"I'll take care of you, angel." I paused. "You done this before?"

"I'm not a virgin."

I made a humming sound, then pushed a thick finger inside her. She made a choked sound. Damn, she was tight. "My cock is way bigger than my finger, sweetheart."

Her cheeks flushed and she lifted her chin. "I can take you."

There was that grit.

She rocked against my hand, and I thrust another finger inside her, stretching her. In, out. In, out. She was panting now, and I worked another finger inside her until she moaned. I needed her to come. I didn't want to hurt her when I fucked her.

She was riding my hand wildly now.

"That's it, angel. Look at you. So damn sexy." I found her clit with my thumb and stroked.

She jerked, her breathing getting faster. Her hands were gripping my shoulders hard, and I knew her nails would leave marks.

"I want you to come now," I told her.

"It usually...takes me a while."

But I could feel her body tensing. She wasn't far away. "Not this time. Not with me."

I pushed my fingers deeper and pinched her clit.

She exploded for me.

She gasped my name, her pussy clenching on my fingers as she shuddered through her release.

"*Oh, God*. Beau." Her head dropped back, exposing her long neck. She let out a throaty cry.

I held her up as she kept coming. When she was done, she stood there, panting hard.

Damn, I wanted to kiss her. Instead, I pulled my hand free of her body, then lifted my fingers to my mouth. Her molten gaze stayed locked on me as I licked her musky sweetness.

"Turn around, sweetheart. I want to see that ass." My voice was rough and edged with a desire that had my cock harder than steel.

She turned, and leaned forward a little, putting the sweet curves of her ass on display. I leaned forward and pressed a kiss to her spine.

"Beau..."

"Like that?" I shaped my hands over her ass, then delved one hand between her legs to her swollen pussy. She made another husky sound and bent forward more. "Yeah, you like that."

My throbbing cock was trapped in my jeans and hurting. Hungry, I reached out and flicked opened my zipper. I lifted my hips and my heavy cock sprung free.

"Hold on, sweet angel." I fished out my wallet and pulled out a condom.

She looked back over one slim shoulder, and her eyes went wide.

"Oh my God, you're huge." Her gaze was locked on my cock. "Everywhere."

I rolled the condom on. "I am." I gripped my cock and pumped it. "All because of you."

She bit her lip.

"You can take me, angel. Right?"

She nodded.

I gripped her hips and pulled her back. "Now, sit on my cock."

"*God.*" She lowered her body, her hands gripping my knees and twisting in the denim.

I guided her where she needed to go, and the sight almost made me spill. *Damn.*

The head of my cock touched warm flesh.

She let out a harsh expulsion of air.

"Ready to take me?" My tone was guttural.

"Yes." She lowered some more, my cock sliding inside her. She moaned. "You're so big. You're stretching me."

I looked, watching the way she took me, the way she stretched for me.

A groan ripped out of my throat.

"*Beau.*"

I pushed her down until I was all the way inside her, her ass hitting my thighs. "You feel so good, Bell."

"*Please...*" Her breaths were coming fast.

"You need more?"

She gave a frantic nod.

I gripped her waist and worked her up and down.

Dammit. She was so tight. All of me ached for her—gut, cock, balls. I wanted to slam her down, but I tried to keep a grip on my control. I reached up and pulled the tie from her hair, and the brown locks fell around her shoulders.

Soon, she was rocking into me, meeting my thrusts.

"*Yes.*" She rocked down on my thighs. "*Beau.*"

I reached around and found her slick clit again. I rubbed it firmly.

She made a choked sound. "I think I'm—"

She came hard again, her pussy milking me. Her body shook.

"So damn sexy." I thrust my hips up, my control shot. I slammed up, filling her. "Fuck, my cock likes being inside you, Bell."

I came, growling her name.

Everything blurred until there was just a rush of hard, hot pleasure.

She collapsed back against me. My cock was still inside her, and she was all soft and slick in my arms.

"My good, sexy girl." I kissed her neck. I wanted to kiss her lips.

But that was against the rules.

She let out a satisfied sigh. "Is it okay if I use your shower?"

"No."

She blinked and looked back. "Why?"

I turned her face and gripped her chin. "Because I'm not done with you yet."

Shifting, I pushed her flat on her back on the bed. A smile bloomed on her lips, and her gaze

CLAIM

traced over the tattoos on my chest. "Oh, well, okay."

I WOKE up to light seeping around the curtains.

Thank fuck the rain had passed. It had hammered down most of the night. I smoothed a hand over the small bed, searching for Bell's slim, toned body.

She'd been a revelation.

Sweet and sexy.

Shy but bold and hungry.

A breath of fresh air. I hadn't felt this turned on, hadn't wanted someone this much, in a long time.

The bed was empty, the sheets cool.

I sat up.

"Dammit." I was alone in the bed.

I glanced around the room. The bathroom door was ajar, and it was empty. I knew she was gone.

Her clothes were gone. Her backpack was gone.

"*Damn.*" I slapped a hand down on the pillows, and heard the crinkle of paper.

There was a note resting on the other pillow.

I lifted it and studied the no nonsense handwriting.

Thank you. For the best night I've had in...well, maybe ever.

Be well, Beau

—Bell.

My fingers curled, crumpling the note. My gut was hard. I wanted to race outside and find her. To make sure she was all right and safe.

I blew out a breath.

But I knew she was long gone. On the bus to Florida.

And I'd never see her again.

I didn't even know her last name.

Hell, I didn't even think Bell was her real name.

I fought through the unfamiliar feelings filling my chest, then carefully folded the note. "Stay safe, angel."

5

BELL

One month later

I strode briskly down the street. I'd been right. I liked New Orleans.

It had a charm, a panache, that I loved. There was always music and the smell of delicious food cooking everywhere I walked.

This street in the Warehouse District was no different.

The old, brick buildings were all renovated, many painted in vibrant colors. Some bars and cafés were doing a brisk business nearby. I saw a couple leaning against their bicycles as they ate huge sandwiches outside a sandwich shop.

The breeze caught my hair, and I pushed it back behind my ear. I knew I should have tied it up today. But when I'd pulled on the cute, green corduroy jacket I'd nabbed for a steal at a local thrift shop, I'd wanted to leave my hair down for once.

I turned the corner.

There was a busy bar on the corner. The sign above the door said Smokehouse, and on the patio, a group of men and woman all talked and laughed, sharing drinks. Next, I passed the closed doors to Ember. I'd heard about the hottest club in the city, though I guessed it wouldn't open until later, when the sun set and the party really started in the Big Easy.

These businesses were owned by Dante Fury—one of the legendary Fury brothers.

In the week I'd been in New Orleans, I'd heard plenty about the Fury brothers. I'd seen Dante's picture, along with his girlfriend's, in the newspaper. He was darkly handsome. I had no idea what his brothers looked like, but apparently, they'd all met in foster care. I was sure they were all impressive.

I stepped in front of the building on the corner and stopped. Nerves flitted through my stomach. Even though the glass door was closed, I could hear the distant sounds of grunts, and the thud of music. I slid my hands into the pockets of my jeans.

Hard Burn. The best gym in the city for learning to fight. I'd read about the owner—Beauden Fury. His bio said he'd been in the military, then he'd been a mercenary, then he'd become a boxing champion. There had been a small picture of him with the article that showed him from the back. He'd been wearing boxing gear with Fury emblazoned on the back of his silky, black robe and his dark head bowed.

Even without seeing his face, I'd felt the strength ebbing from him.

I touched my arm, rubbing it gently. I needed the best. I needed to learn to fight and defend myself.

Because the nightmare hunting me had found me again.

A mix of emotions filled me: fear, terror, anger, helplessness, and a choking sense of unfairness.

I wanted to tip my head back and cry, "Why me?"

But I stuffed those emotions all the way down and dragged in a deep breath. Playing the victim never helped.

I'd be no one's victim.

Especially not Carr's.

I pushed open the door to Hard Burn and stepped inside.

The sounds of fighting were louder, along with the throb of music. There were lots of boxing rings, each one defined by red ropes, although not many with people in them. I guessed it was too early in the day. There were a few people at the back of the gym, lifting weights. I saw one big guy in a sweat-stained tank holding onto two long ropes, lifting his arms up and down.

I figured that once people finished work, Hard Burn would be full.

As I stepped farther inside, smells hit me—sweat, deodorant, and the sweet undertone of a cleaning product. I fiddled with my hair. I was currently back to my natural black again. I sighed. But not for long. I dyed my hair every month, but this month, I'd just wanted some little piece of the old me.

For a second, I thought of the only night where for a few glorious hours, I'd felt happy, safe, and normal.

Those hours in a cheap motel on the Louisiana border.

I shivered.

I'd relived every single moment of the hours I'd spent with Beau so many times, often with my fingers between my legs. I dragged in a breath. I couldn't afford to daydream. Today, I had to focus on the future me. The one who could fight and defend herself.

Beauden Fury was the best, and I needed him.

"You lost, girly?"

I turned to see an older man—probably in his late fifties or early sixties—staring at me. He had a bald head, and what I guessed was some Latino heritage. His dark brown eyes regarded me steadily.

"I'm here to see Beauden Fury."

The man's dark brows rose. "He know you're coming?"

I tried not to fidget. "No."

The man sniffed. "You're too young, girly. He's not a fan of the boxing groupies."

What? It took me a few seconds to realize what he meant. Beauden Fury must have women coming looking for him a lot.

"No. I want to learn to fight."

The man cocked his head. "Well, then. My name's Gio."

"I'm Bellamy." Or at least I was now.

"All right, Bellamy, I can share our class timetables with you—"

I shook my head. "I need to learn to fight. I need Beauden Fury to teach me."

Now, the man's brow creased. "He don't give many private lessons, and only with experienced fighters."

Desperation and despair welled inside me. If I couldn't fight, Carr would kill me.

Gio must've seen some emotion on my face. His expression warmed a little with sympathy. "Look, why don't we talk over some options—"

I shook my head. "I shouldn't have come."

I had no idea what to do next.

If I couldn't fight, what were my options?

Keep running.

Keep surviving.

Keep being hunted.

I took a step backward.

Gio held out a hand. "Don't go, girly. Let's talk. I'll make you a coffee." He glanced back over his shoulder and something like relief filled his features. "Better yet, why don't you talk with Beauden? He'll give you good advice, whatever problems are chasing you."

Lifting my head, I looked past Gio to the man striding through the gym.

He'd clearly just showered, and was wearing black athletic shorts and no shirt. He had a T-shirt in his hand.

My mouth went dry.

He had powerful, muscular legs, and thick slabs of muscle over his abs and broad chest. All of it was covered in ink. His brawny arms were also covered in tattoos. A mix of flowers, swirls, and geometric patterns.

I froze. My brain stopped working.

It was ink I knew. Tattoos I'd traced with my tongue.

My head jerked up. I got the impression of thick,

shaggy black hair, but my gaze was locked on the rugged face that had haunted my dreams. Those familiar gray eyes.

Beau.

My Beau was Beauden Fury.

6

BEAU

I couldn't fucking believe it.

Bell.

Bell was in my gym.

I stood there, shirt clenched in my grip and stared back at her.

For twenty-eight long days, I'd thought of her—when I woke in the morning, when I was training, when I sat alone in my apartment above Hard Burn. When I jerked off.

I'd prayed she was safe. I'd hated not knowing.

Her hair was black now and loose around her shoulders. I could tell it was a natural color. It suited her better.

She was still too pale, and looked thinner.

I saw panic skitter across her features. She took two steps back.

I strode forward, yanked my T-shirt over my head, and closed the distance between us. The rest of the gym became a blur. I only saw Bell and her big, blue eyes.

"Bell," I growled.

"I was leaving."

"No, you're not."

I gripped her forearm, and she winced. I instantly loosened my grip. I knew my strength, and I was always careful. My grasp shouldn't have hurt her.

Gio blinked. "You two know each other?"

"Yes."

"No," Bell said.

Gio cleared his throat. "Bellamy wants to learn to fight."

"Bellamy," I said slowly, tasting her full name.

"I shouldn't be here," she whispered.

"Too late. Gio, we'll be in my office."

I took Bell's hand and towed her to my office. Once we were inside, I closed the door.

She looked around, her eyebrows rising. "This is your office? You work in here?"

Okay, it was messy. There were piles of papers on the desk, and half covering the laptop I did my best to avoid. I knew I had a bunch of invoices in there somewhere that I had to deal with. The couch in the corner of the space was old, with a faded plaid pattern. It was ugly, but I'd had the thing from when I'd first started Hard Burn. It had sentimental value.

I faced her. "Why are you here? How did you find me?"

She got a pinched look and ran a hand through her hair. "I didn't know this gym was yours. I didn't know you were Beauden Fury."

"You didn't answer my question." I leaned back

against the desk.

She fidgeted. "I need to learn to fight."

"Why?"

She got a stubborn look. "Because."

So many damn secrets. I could smell that maddening perfume of hers. Sometimes I woke up thinking I could smell her on my sheets.

"I thought you were going to Florida?"

She shrugged a shoulder. "I made it. Just. To Pensacola." She reached over and tidied a stack of papers on my desk.

"Why did you run out on me?" I demanded.

She looked up, her lips parted.

I felt my gut tighten. Those were lips that I'd wanted to kiss, but hadn't been allowed to. That night, I'd had to settle for sliding my cock between them.

And now I was getting hard. *Shit.*

"Our night together was over." She fiddled with the end of her hair. "I had a bus to catch. I didn't want to make it awkward."

"Nothing about the time we spent together was awkward, Bell."

Her cheeks flushed. It felt like the air in the office got warm. Both of us were very aware of each other.

She licked her lips. "It was... It was good, Beau. I didn't want to ruin those perfect hours."

Damn, this woman killed me. So distrusting, yet yearning for connection. She was the kind of woman I usually steered well clear of.

She deserved so much better than me.

But right now, she was afraid of something, or someone, and I wanted to help her.

If she was in danger…

That was one thing I wouldn't stand for. And it was one thing I could help her with.

"Why do you want to learn to fight?"

"For protection. I'm a woman who's on my own. I need some skills."

There was more to it, although I doubted she'd share. She reminded me of a prickly little porcupine.

As I watched her, she glanced away. Her gaze traced over the tattoos on my arm.

I couldn't have her here. I shouldn't have touched someone so young and fresh in the first place.

She wasn't for me.

I was a rough foster kid-turned-merc-turned boxer. I was rough, tough, and tattooed. That creamy skin of hers had never been touched by ink. I knew, because I'd checked every inch of it.

The reality was, we had chemistry. That one night together had proven that. I'd never come quicker, harder, or so often.

If she was here, in my orbit, in my space, I'd take her again. I wouldn't be able to help myself.

I cleared my throat. "We have a good self-defense class for women."

I saw Bell stiffen.

"Shay, the instructor, is really good. She has lots of experience."

Bell shook her head. "No. I want *you* to teach me to fight."

"That's not a good idea."

7

BELL

I still couldn't believe it.

Beau, *my* Beau, was Beauden Fury.

The Fury brothers had fought their way from a life as foster kids, to successful businessmen. They were all rich, owned countless properties and businesses, attended the best parties in New Orleans, women wanted them.

Beau was right there. I could reach out and touch him.

His hard muscles were covered by soft cotton now, and his shirt had the Hard Burn logo on it—a boxing glove covered in flames. I looked up at his black beard and gray eyes, then my gaze fell to his hands. I remembered how it felt to have those hands on me.

"Shay's a really good trainer," Beau said. "All the women who attend love her classes—"

I clicked into his words. My mouth flattened. He didn't want to train me. He probably didn't want me anywhere near him.

I was just his accidental one-night stand.

"I don't want some beginner class. I need the best."

"Bell..." There was resignation in his voice.

I stepped back. "I shouldn't have come." I let out a harsh laugh. "Of course you wouldn't want to teach me."

I headed for the door of his office.

"Bell—" He grabbed my arm.

"I'm leaving."

"No. Not like this." He spun me around. "Come to a class. Try it out."

"It's you or no one." I'd have to find someone else.

But the reality was that I'd need to move on and leave New Orleans. I'd have to give up the room I'd found in the old, graceful mansion turned boarding house. And I couldn't go back to the cash work washing dishes at the Italian restaurant near the French Quarter.

I needed to run again. Put more space between me and Carr.

I could already feel him breathing down my neck.

Once I found a new city, then I'd find another trainer to teach me to fight. One who wasn't as tempting as Beauden Fury.

One who didn't turn me on by just looking at him.

I tugged on my arm. "Let me go."

"I want some answers first."

I yanked free. "My life is none of your business."

His face hardened. "It became my business the first time I slid my cock inside you. It was definitely my business the second time I did it."

A shot of heat—and anger—hit my belly. "It was a one-night stand. It didn't mean anything."

"Bullshit." He gripped my forearm again.

Ignoring the sting of pain, I whipped my other arm out, forming a fist. I punched his gut.

It was like hitting rock. He shifted, and I wrenched my arm free and knocked him away.

"You know some basics," he said.

I nodded. Over the last year, I'd taken some classes and private lessons when I could afford them. "But I need more than that."

Snake fast, he grabbed my arm.

This time I couldn't hide my wince.

His brows drew together and before I knew what he was doing, he shoved the sleeve of my jacket up. The fading bruises were clear in the bright, florescent light. They weren't pretty.

Now storms gathered in his eyes.

"Who did this?" he demanded.

It was easy to make out the finger marks. From a large hand.

"Another asshole who thought he could boss me around."

Beau's gaze hardened. "I'd never hurt you. Or any other woman." His tone was frigid. "Anyone who hurts someone weaker or less strong than them deserves the worst."

My chest squeezed. The look in his eye told me that he'd gone somewhere else. That he was speaking from experience.

Not that I could ever imagine Beau being weaker or less strong than anybody. But I guessed foster care wasn't all roses and rainbows. Being alone as an adult was hard enough, being alone as a child...

I pushed my sleeve down. "I know. I'm sorry. This asshole, well, I have *no* plans to let him hurt me again."

Or kill me. I didn't mention that bit to Beau.

I turned and started to open the door, but a big hand pressed against the wood and closed it again, before I could leave.

I stared at the door, and felt Beau's big body behind mine.

I'd forgotten how much heat he put off, and I soaked it in. I felt his face brush against my hair.

"I like your hair black."

I swallowed. "It's my natural color. But I have to dye it frequently."

"To stay hidden."

I didn't reply. It wasn't really a question anyway.

"Don't you want to stop running?"

I quivered and turned. Our faces were an inch apart.

"Of course I do, but I don't have that luxury, not until I know I can fight him off."

Beau's jaw worked. "You don't need to do this alone."

"Yes, I do." Because Chandler Carr was an animal. He'd hunt down anyone and everyone I cared about. "I have to protect myself."

8

BEAU

I 'd never wanted anyone's secrets before.

But staring into Bellamy's face, I wanted hers. Deep inside, I felt her driving need to protect herself.

I hated not knowing who she was afraid of.

"Who?" I demanded.

She looked to the side and didn't respond.

"Who is he?"

She shook her head.

I felt a burn of frustration. *Dammit*. I watched a stubborn look settle on her face.

"Is Bellamy your real name?"

She hesitated. "No. But it's close."

Well, that was something, at least.

There was a knock at the door. It opened a few inches and one of my trainers, Chris, poked his head in.

"Hey, Beau, I need some new mats for—" He spotted Bell. "Oh, sorry."

I lifted my chin. "I'm busy, Chris. Get whatever you need, and I'll catch you later."

"Sure. Sorry again." He closed the door.

Bell edged away from me.

"How long have you been in New Orleans?" I asked.

"One week."

I looked at her arm. The bruises were hidden now, but the sight of them was burned into my brain.

"And he found you?"

"Not here. Not yet. The place I was before, after..."

After our night together.

"You got a place to stay?"

She nodded.

"It safe?"

Another nod.

"Job?" I continued.

"Cash work at a restaurant."

That wouldn't pay much. I didn't let myself think, I just went with my gut. "You can work here. Clean up around the gym, ensure towels and stock are kept up, do other odd jobs."

That stubborn look intensified. "I don't need a pity job."

"I've been meaning to hire someone. Gio's been on my back about it. You a decent worker?"

"Yes."

"Then you work here." Where she'd be protected from whatever asshole was after her.

Was it an ex-boyfriend? I hated that idea, and my hands flexed. Whoever he was, I hoped I got the chance to meet him.

"And Bell, our first fight lesson starts tomorrow after your shift."

Her face changed. "You'll teach me?"

"Yes." Against my better judgment. But there was no way in hell I was going to let her disappear again. Not when someone was after her.

"Thank you." Her voice was drenched with relief.

I cleared my throat. "What happened before, between us, is in the past. The job and lessons come with no strings attached."

A smile flirted on her mouth. "Told you that you're a good guy."

"I'm not."

She grinned. "Are, too."

I pointed to the door. "Get out before I change my mind. Talk to Gio. He'll give you a uniform and your shift times."

She headed for the door.

"Wait."

She turned.

"You got a cellphone?" I asked.

She nodded.

I snatched up a scrap of paper off my desk and scrawled my cell number on it. I handed it to her. "If you need anything, you call me."

She took the paper and worked it through her fingers. "Okay."

"Bell, I mean it."

She nodded. "Thanks, Beau."

She walked out, and I leaned against the doorframe and watched her stop to talk with Gio. As she left the gym, I noticed two guys sparring in a ring stop to watch her. She had a graceful way of walking that caught the eye.

I scowled and swallowed the need to tell them to get their eyes off her, and focus on their damn fight.

She wasn't mine.

I had to resist the temptation.

Gio stepped up beside me. "You're going to train her."

"Yeah."

"She's in trouble."

"She is, but she won't talk about it." Not yet.

"And you gave her a job." The other man was watching me, a brow arched.

"So?"

"So, you can't keep your eyes off her."

I snorted. "She's way too young for me."

"But you have a history."

"Not really. We just met once." And I'd touched every part of her and fucked her brains out.

Gio grunted. He didn't sound convinced.

"Don't you have work to do?" I said sharply.

The older man held up his hands and walked off muttering to himself.

I rubbed the back of my neck. I needed to keep my hands off Bellamy.

I pulled my cellphone out, stared at it for a second, then touched a button. I pressed the phone to my ear.

A sultry female voice answered. "Hello."

"Hi, Klara. This is Beauden. Are you free for dinner tomorrow night?"

9

BELL

I bustled around my small room, getting ready for my first shift at Hard Burn.

The room was tiny, but it did the job. There was a single bed, and an adjoining bathroom the size of a postage stamp. The elegant, old mansion was on the edge of the Garden District. Someone had split the big home up into multiple rooms that were now rented out individually. The lady who ran it was tough but fair. She only rented to women.

The best thing about it was that I could catch the streetcar into the French Quarter and the Warehouse District. It was easy for me to get to Hard Burn.

I fingered the embroidered boxing glove logo on my polo shirt. A part of me still couldn't believe that Beau was Beauden Fury.

And he'd given me a job and promised to teach me to fight.

I drew in a breath, determination filling me. With

Beau's help, I could fight off Carr. I'd finally have a chance.

After tightening my ponytail, I snatched up my backpack and headed out. I locked my door and headed down the hall. The old floorboards creaked under foot. The main staircase was graceful, with a smooth, carved handrail. The entire house made me think of a stately old lady.

A blonde woman was jogging up the stairs.

"Oh, hey, Bell." She smiled at me.

"Hi, Maggie. Did you just get off shift?"

"Sure did." Maggie huffed out a breath. "It was a *crazy* night at the hospital."

Maggie was a nurse whose room was three doors down from mine. I'd met her the first day I'd moved in, and her bubbly personality reminded me of Allie.

"Hope you sleep well."

"I will if Natalie in the room beside mine doesn't have her music blaring. Again." The blonde's gaze dropped to my shirt. "You get a new job?"

I nodded. "At a gym."

"That isn't just any gym. It's one that's owned by one of the Fury brothers. I heard the waitlist to train there is huge." Maggie waggled her eyebrows. "Is Beauden Fury as gorgeous as they say? Big, muscled, covered in ink?"

My belly spasmed. I really didn't like Maggie drooling over Beau. "He's the boss, but yes, he's all those things."

Maggie let out a gusty sigh. "He must have all kinds of beautiful women lined up, but a girl can dream. Catch you later, Bell."

I headed down the stairs and through the entry. Did Beau have a line of women? I worried my bottom lip, my stomach doing an unhappy flip. Gio had initially thought I was a groupie.

With a shake of my head, I shoved those thoughts away. Outside, the day was sunny with a few clouds dotting the sky. The weather was definitely cooling off, but I didn't need my jacket.

It was a quick walk to the streetcar stop and one arrived a few minutes later. I paid for my fare, then found a seat, and smiled. The streetcars were another part of the New Orleans charm.

For a second, I could almost imagine I was just a normal woman, heading off to work, with nothing to worry about.

But I wasn't. I stared out at the sidewalk as it rushed past.

I'd learn to fight, but I wouldn't abuse Beau's decent nature. He wanted to help me, but there was no way I'd drag him into my mess. I had to stay alone. I couldn't let myself forget that.

Finally, the streetcar neared my stop. It was only a short few blocks away from Hard Burn.

After thanking the driver, I hopped off. When I looked up, I saw the shadow of a man in the doorway of a warehouse nearby.

He was watching me.

The hairs on the back of my neck rose. *No.* My pulse skittered. Carr couldn't have found me already.

I stood there, feet frozen to the concrete. I couldn't

see the man's face. He was hidden in the shadows. Some people passed in front of me, blocking my view.

When I looked back, I saw a man emerge from the warehouse, waving at a couple heading in his direction. They hugged, then set off down the street.

It wasn't him. I scanned the warehouse and saw no more shadows.

I blew out a breath, forcing myself to relax. I was seeing boogeymen everywhere.

"It wasn't Carr, Bell," I murmured to myself. "You're fine."

Still, as I headed toward Hard Burn, I walked a little faster than usual.

10

BEAU

I blocked the fist coming my way, and hammered a jab into my opponent's arm.

He grunted.

I bounced back, enjoying the sweat on my skin and my warm, loose muscles. There was nothing like a good fight to clear the head.

Boxing had given me that so many times. It had saved me.

After my time as a mercenary, and my rotten childhood, shit had built up. I could've chosen drugs, booze, and sex to drown in, but instead, I'd chosen to climb into the ring.

To train, learn to assess my opponents, then learn the strategy of the fight.

It had kept me sane.

And my brothers had kept me grounded.

"Damn, Beauden, you hit like a freight train."

Across from me, Dante rubbed his shoulder.

I raised a brow. "You're not giving up, are you?"

My brother's jaw tightened. "Fuck, no."

He came at me in a flurry of punches. We moved across the ring, and I fell into the fight. I was barely aware of Colton and Kavner fighting in the next ring beside us. Or Reath running on the treadmill in the main gym area. My brothers and I worked out together a few times a week.

But I noticed the second Bell walked into the gym.

She was wearing black leggings and a black Hard Burn polo shirt that Gio had given her. Her black hair was up in a high ponytail.

She looked so damn young.

While I was distracted, Dante punched me in the side of the head.

The asshole grinned at me. "The first rule you taught me was not to get distracted in the ring."

"Fuck you." I rubbed my jaw. "And I'd be careful, because you don't want me to mess up that face of yours. Mila wouldn't be happy."

"She loves me however I come."

Dante said that with a touch of awe. Like he couldn't quite believe how much his girlfriend adored him.

I felt...something. No one had ever felt that way about me. Certainly not my parents. I'd been a burden to them, and then later, a potential paycheck.

I slapped my gloves together. I tried not to think of the people who'd birthed me. Neither of them deserved the time or energy.

Glancing to the side, I saw Bell wave at Gio. He stopped to talk to her. I'd told him to give her a tour and show her the ropes.

"Who's the girl?" Dante asked.

"Woman. If Shay hears you calling her a girl, she'll knock your teeth out."

Dante eyed Bell. "She's almost a girl."

"New hire. She's going to do odd jobs around the gym."

"Not your usual choice of employee. Most of your guys are boxers."

"She needed a job."

Dante swiped his arm across his sweaty forehead. "I smell a story."

I pulled my gloves off. "No story."

"She's a person in some sort of need. All your guys are, starting with Gio."

Gio had been an old trainer of mine back in my early fighting days. We'd lost contact, then he'd gone through a bad divorce, and ended up battling alcoholism. He'd lost his job, his wife, his house, and was scraping the bottom of the barrel.

I'd given him a chance when no one else would. It was all he'd needed. Now, he was my most loyal employee, and he knew the gym inside and out.

"I'm not sure of her story," I told Dante. "She's on the run from something." I watched her. "Or rather, someone."

"You guys done?" Colt was leaning on the ropes of the next ring, Kavner beside him.

They made a pair. Colt, the tall, grumpy bounty hunter with tats on his arms, and Kav, the glossy, handsome businessman.

I nodded. "Yep."

"Who wants a round with me?" Reath appeared with a towel around his neck and sweat slicking his brown skin.

"I will," I said.

That's when I realized Bell was walking toward us. I stiffened.

"Now, who's this?" Kav murmured.

"Beau's new hire," Dante said. "But I'm pretty sure there's more to it."

I ignored them.

"Hi," Bell said brightly, her gaze on me.

"Hey." I ran a hand through my damp hair and knew I smelled like sweat. "Bellamy, these are my brothers. Guys, this is Bellamy."

Bell blinked and looked at them all. "Hello."

I pointed to them one by one. "Dante, Kavner, Colt, and the one beside you is Reath."

Beside her, Reath smiled.

She stared at him, and my gut tightened. Reath was handsome. We'd been giving him shit about being pretty his entire life. He made up for it by being a badass. He was former Army and CIA, and ran Phoenix Security Services—the best security firm in New Orleans.

"It's nice to meet you." She gave them a small smile. "I hope there's not a test to remember everybody's names."

"You'll get to know us." Kav smiled. "We're around here pretty often. Now, I need to go." He climbed out of the ring. "My lovely London is waiting for me."

Bell held up a cloth and a bottle of spray. "And I need to get to work." She headed for the gym equipment, and I watched her go. Her leggings hugged her toned legs and ass.

"You like her."

I whipped my head around and looked at Reath. "Yeah. She's nice."

"No, you *like* her."

Reath had always seen too damn much.

"She's a little young," Kav said.

I managed to swallow my growl.

"Shit, Reath," Dante said, gaze locked on my face. "You're right. He likes her."

"Don't you assholes have places to be?" I climbed out of the ring. "Businesses to run. Women to get henpecked by."

Dante snorted. "I'm telling Mila you said she henpecks."

"Hey, I thought we were fighting?" Reath complained.

Kav stroked his jaw. "I think things are going to get interesting around here."

11

BELL

I finished stacking freshly laundered towels on the shelves. Evening had fallen, and the gym had gotten really busy. There were some amazing fighters who were training. Some of them with Beau, some with his other trainers—Chris and Pedro—whom I'd met earlier in the day.

Beau was tough. I watched him whenever I could. He pushed them hard, and they all respected him.

The women's self-defense class was just finishing up. Shay, the instructor, was a fit blonde in her thirties and was in excellent shape. I peered through the glass into the room. Shay's cropped tank showed off her killer abs as she demonstrated a move. The class was full, and she had their rapt attention.

They'd done some good stuff, but I needed more. I needed to know how to fight off a killer.

The man who'd killed Allison.

Grief for my best friend washed over me. She'd been stolen far too soon.

Women started heading out of the room, laughing and chatting. They were all flushed and coated with perspiration. A woman with her brown hair in two thick braids came out, wiping her face with a towel. She spotted me, then headed over.

"You must be Bell."

"I am."

"Gio told me you'd started working here which is *great*. This place needs some more female staff." She smiled, and I guessed she was around my age. "I'm Karina, and I'm here like four or five times a week. I'm on a bit of a health kick at the moment." She ran a hand down her blue leggings. "Damn five pounds I can never shift."

I thought her curves looked great.

"Now, I can already tell we're going to be friends," Karina continued. "I'll be here tomorrow morning, and I'll bring you one of my world-famous green smoothies."

Karina kept talking and didn't seem to need much input from me. I did think a green smoothie sounded kind of gross.

She gripped my arm and squeezed. "Can't wait to get to know you better, Bell. See you tomorrow." She waved as she headed for the change rooms.

I blinked, feeling a little like I'd been caught in a whirlwind.

"You'll get used to her."

I turned and saw Shay standing there. Again, I felt envy for her formidable abs. The instructor drank from a water bottle.

"So, what's your story, Bell?"

"Um...no story. Beau just offered me a job."

"Oh, there's a story. There's always a story with the people Beau collects. Gio had hit rock bottom, Chris had suffered a traumatic brain injury in the ring, Pedro's business had gone bankrupt." Shay paused. "I'd just escaped an abusive relationship."

I gasped. I couldn't imagine this fit, strong woman being abused.

"It can happen to anyone," the other woman murmured. "Now, I help women make themselves safe." She cocked her head. "I think you know something about that. I know the look."

I lifted a shoulder. "A little. Beau's going to teach me to fight."

Shay's eyebrows winged up. "Beau's going to train you?"

I nodded.

"Wow. There are people all around the country who'd kill for that opportunity." She studied me. "Interesting."

I fought the urge to fidget.

"Well, good luck, Bell. You ever want to try my class, you're always welcome." With a nod, Shay headed for the change rooms.

With the noise of the gym echoing in my ears, I turned and scanned around. Apparently, it was a big deal that Beau had agreed to train me.

He's just a good guy, Bell.

And it sounded like he had a thing for helping out people in need.

"Hey, you daydreaming?"

I looked up at Gio. The old man had been friendly, in his own gruff sort of way. He'd shown me every part of the gym, including the stairs at the back that led up to Beau's apartment. He lived above the gym.

"Time for your lesson." Gio jerked his head toward a ring. "Better get moving."

"Sorry." I jolted. When I looked over, I saw Beauden standing in a ring at the back, well away from the others. He was watching me.

"Go." Gio shooed me away.

I headed over.

"Come on." Beau held the ropes apart for me to climb in. "How was your first day?"

"Great." It had been. I'd enjoyed the work. Even the cleaning.

"Good. These are for you." He held up a set of cloth wrappings and a pair of blue boxing gloves. "Should be the right size."

They were far smaller than his red ones hanging on the ropes.

I took them and frowned. "These gloves are new." Having spent some time dusting off the merchandise at the front desk today, I knew exactly what the wraps and gloves cost.

"They're yours," Beau said.

"I can't afford them."

"Consider them a gift to welcome you to the Hard Burn team."

I fought the urge to hand them back. I hated being indebted to anyone, or accepting charity.

"If you want to fight, you need them."

He was right. I nodded. "Thank you."

"Then let's get started."

I unrolled the wraps. I'd been watching people do them all day. I started wrapping up my first hand.

After about four seconds, a pair of big hands grabbed mine. Beau took over, wrapping my hands with practiced moves.

His fingers brushed my skin, and I felt the touch all the way up my arm.

Get a grip, Bell.

"Here you go." He held out one of the boxing gloves and I slid it on. It was the perfect size. He held up the glove for my other hand.

Once they were on, I turned my hands, getting used to the feel of them.

"Right." He picked up two black pads and slipped them onto his hands. "These are focus pads. These are your targets so we can practice your hits and build your power."

I nodded.

"We'll go through some basic hits."

"So you won't use your gloves?"

"You're not ready to fight yet, Bell. You have to learn to walk before you can run."

I blew out a breath. "Okay." I lifted my gloves.

"Let's adjust this stance first." He moved in beside me, touching my elbow and moving my arms into place. "You need power in these arms. No noodles." He gave my arm a shake.

I tensed my muscles and focused.

He stepped in front of me and held up the pads. "We're going to learn jab, hook, cross, and uppercut."

"I know all the basic punches."

"Good. Show me. Let's go."

We slowly worked through the moves. I slammed my gloves into his pads. He'd call out a punch, and I'd follow through. Soon, I got the feel for it, my blood humming. He started to speed up, and then added different combos.

My world reduced down to Beau's deep voice and those focus pads—my targets.

Smack. Smack. Smack.

Soon, I was sweating, and trying to increase the power of my hits.

"Again," Beau barked.

I wiped my forearm across my head, and went again. *Jab, jab, cross. Jab, cross, left hook. Uppercut, cross, left hook.*

I got it wrong a few times, and gritted my teeth. But soon, we had a rhythm.

Then, on my next swing, I overbalanced and stumbled forward. I slammed into Beau.

He caught me, but now I was too focused on the feel of him, the smell of him. I wanted to curl up against his chest and stay right there.

"You okay?" He looked down at me.

I managed a nod.

"Good." He stepped back. "Again."

I swallowed a groan.

For the next combos, he moved around the ring. I followed, slamming my gloves into the pads. He whirled past me, and our bodies brushed.

I sucked in a breath, and managed to connect my gloves with the pad.

Focus on the fight, Bell, not him.

On the next combo, we came close again. So close that I sensed every bit of that big, muscular body. I was slick between my legs, and it had nothing to do with perspiration.

"Uppercut," he ordered.

I moved forward and slammed my glove up into his pad.

We paused. I was only an inch from him, and I felt like I was on fire. I glanced up at his face.

I saw pride on his rugged features, then as he met my gaze, I saw an answering flicker of heat.

Then he stepped back. "You did well, Bell."

I felt a flush of pleasure. "Thanks."

He pulled the focus pads off. "Go take a shower. You'll be sore tomorrow. The hot water will help."

I nodded. I floated to the ladies' change room.

We'd had our first training session. I was learning to fight.

The change room was empty, and I got my backpack out of the locker, then hurried to a shower stall. I stood under the hot water.

My skin felt like it was on fire, my belly swirling with desire. I imagined Beau with me in the gym. It was just the two of us. Him taking me down to the mats, pinning me there.

His big cock sliding inside me.

I moaned, aroused by the water on my skin, the feel of being close to Beau, the memories of that night we'd spent together. I slid a hand over my belly and between my legs. I wanted Beauden. I wanted him so much.

I rubbed my slick clit. It didn't take long for a quick flash of an orgasm to hit me. I bit my lip, moaning his name in my head.

Then I pressed my hand to the cool tiles.

I wanted him. Could we find a way to train and fuck? It would be mutually beneficial to both of us.

For however long I was in New Orleans, maybe I could have one good thing for myself.

I was going to talk to him.

I turned off the water and dried off, my head filled with pictures of me and Beau. I pulled on some fresh clothes—jeans and a long-sleeved T-shirt in a pretty green. The jeans were a thrift shop bargain, but my mom had given me the shirt. I tucked my Hard Burn polo into my backpack, fingering the fabric.

I liked it. It made me feel like I was a part of something.

Heading out, I slung my backpack over my shoulder.

Now, I just had to get up the courage to ask Beau if he was interested in grabbing a drink.

I saw Gio first.

"Hey, good work in the ring, girly. You have potential."

I smiled. "Thanks."

He blinked. "You should do that more often."

"What?"

"Smile."

I felt a blush in my cheeks. "Um, where's Beau? I just wanted to thank him."

"Well, I think the boss is a little busy." Gio nodded toward reception.

I turned, and my smile dropped, hitting my feet.

Beau stood in reception with a tall, curvaceous brunette. He had an arm around her waist, and they were smiling at each other. The woman was wearing a gorgeous wrap dress in a burnt-orange color. I didn't even own a dress anymore. Her long hair was streaked with blonde, and she had a hand pressed to his hard chest.

I felt my insides shrink. I tasted sludge in my mouth.

She was perfect for him. She was probably in her early thirties, tall, and gorgeous.

Not a young, lost woman whose life was a shambles.

I'd been an idiot to think that Beauden Fury would be interested in me for anything other than a convenient one-night stand. And now, I was just someone he felt sorry for.

"—is going out on a date."

I realized that Gio was talking and pasted on a smile. From the look on his face, I knew it must look fake.

"Right, well, I was just going to thank him again. I won't disturb him. I'll just get going."

And get back to my room and bandage up my bleeding wounds from seeing Beau with another woman.

A woman who'd touch his hard muscles, and trace his tattoos. Who'd kiss him.

Something I'd never done.

And would never do.

I hurried off toward the front door.

"Girly—?"

"See you tomorrow, Gio."

I kept as much distance between me and the couple at the front desk as I could. I focused my full attention on the door. Just get out the door.

"Bell?"

Beau's voice brought a burst of pain.

I didn't look around, just waved a hand. "Night, boss."

"Bell, wait—"

I shoved open the door and let it close behind me. Then I lifted my head and met his gaze through the glass.

He was frowning at me. Thankfully, his woman had her back to me.

His gaze locked on my face.

Then I turned away and hurried into the night.

Alone. How I had to stay, whether I liked it or not.

12

BEAU

I scrubbed a hand over my face as I headed down to the gym. I hadn't opened this morning, Gio had, and the familiar sounds of workout music, the *thunk* of weights, and the slap of gloves was like a balm.

I'd slept like shit. Mostly thanks to my bad date.

Klara was lovely. She was sexy as hell, successful, easy to talk with.

And I hadn't felt one speck of interest.

It was the reason I hadn't asked her out when she'd first given me her number at a party a few weeks back.

Scrubbing a hand over my face, I walked toward my office. I nodded at my trainer, Chris.

But all I could think about was Bell's face. The way she'd looked at me through the door last night, stricken and hurt.

She tried to hide it, but I'd seen it clearly.

And it had cut.

I was an idiot. Trying to get my mind off one woman

by spending time with another. *Stupid*. It was unfair to both of them.

Then I spotted Bell and slowed.

She was wearing leggings again, and was bent over, cleaning a bench. I couldn't pull my gaze off her ass.

Karina, one of our regulars, called out to her. The women chatted for a moment, and Karina handed Bell a take-out cup. I watched as she gingerly took a sip, then smiled.

Then she turned a little more and saw me. Her smile evaporated.

I set my shoulders back and approached. "Morning, Karina."

"Hey there, Beau." She tossed her braids over her shoulders. "I was just giving Bell one of my world-famous smoothies, now I need to get my workout done, and then head to class."

"You're studying?" Bell asked.

Karina nodded. "Hospitality and tourism management." She tapped the cup in Bell's hand. "Enjoy all that goodness."

As the other woman hurried off, I looked at my new employee. "Morning, Bell."

She nodded, and I saw her glance toward the stairs to my apartment... Like she was waiting for something. Or someone.

"Late night, boss man." Chris slapped my shoulder as he walked past. "The brunette was *stunning*, so I don't blame you."

"Mind your own business." I glanced up and saw that Bell was gone.

My date had ended with me dropping Klara home. I hadn't even kissed her.

Feeling pissed off, I headed for my office.

I paused in the doorway. The papers on my desk were now all in neat piles. I smelled the lingering scent of mangoes. Walking in, I rifled briefly through the paperwork. They were all in order—invoices to be paid, receipts, training notes that I'd written.

I dropped into my chair, and it creaked under my weight. I wanted to find Bell and...

And what, asshole?

My mouth flattened and I opened my laptop. *Work.* What I needed was to get to work.

Bell and I had a training session later. I'd talk to her then.

I shook my head. The real problem was knowing that Bell being unhappy was what was making me this damn unsettled.

I HEADED out of my office, checking my watch. It was time for our training session.

I'd barely seen Bell all day. She'd flittered around the gym, working, and avoiding my office like the plague. Last time I'd seen her, she'd been polishing the glass on the room where Shay held her classes.

"Gio, have you seen Bell?"

"Yeah. She was doing stocktake on the cleaning supplies. She's a good worker."

With a nod, I headed toward the back room.

"Beau?"

I glanced back.

"Don't hurt her." Gio scratched the side of his bald head. "I think she's been hurt enough."

"I'm trying to help her."

"Are you?"

I shot my old friend a look, then went to find Bell.

I found her crouched down in the supply closet, scribbling on a notepad.

"Bellamy?"

She jolted. "Oh, it's you."

Her voice was flat, and she didn't meet my gaze.

"It's time to train. I'll meet you in the ring."

"I'm not finished here—"

"You are now."

She looked up, a stubborn expression on her face.

"You're here to train," I said. "So we train."

She snapped the notepad closed and stood. "Fine."

"Good."

She stomped past me. I watched her disappear into the change room. I reached the ring, and grabbed the focus pads.

A moment later, Bell appeared. She'd switched her Hard Burn shirt for a black tank top, and she had her wraps on her hands. She was carrying her gloves.

She climbed into the ring, again not looking at me.

I sighed. "Bell—"

She shoved her hands into her gloves. "I'm ready. Let's do this."

Right. It seemed talking was not on the agenda.

"Jab, jab, hook," I ordered.

She hit the pads. Hard.

We settled into our training, and every hit was filled with angry power. We circled the ring. "Let's mix things up a bit. You do the hits you want."

Her face sharpened. She came at me with a flurry of hits. Her gloves hit my pads with forceful slaps. I had to use everything I had to get the pads into position in time.

"You're pissed off."

Her chest heaved. "No. I'm training."

She slammed a fist toward my gut. I blocked it.

"Bell, look about Klara—"

Bell whirled and landed more hits. They came so fast I barely blocked them in time.

"I have *no* desire to hear anything about Klara." Her voice was clipped. She swung her arms, coming at me again.

I dumped a pad and grabbed her wrist. "Hey—"

"Let me go." She tried to yank her arm back.

"No."

Suddenly, she hooked her leg around my ankle. I wasn't expecting it. I crashed to the ground, bouncing on the mat, but I didn't let her go. She fell on top of me.

"Let me go." She squirmed.

I gripped Bell's hips. "I didn't sleep with her."

Pure anger filled her face before she hid it. "It's none of my business."

I cupped her cheek. I couldn't stop myself. "I think it is."

She went still, not looking at me.

"I'm sorry," I murmured.

Blue eyes flicked to mine. She yanked her arm free,

and I let her go. She pushed to her feet. "It's none of my business who you fuck, Beau. You can fuck every woman in New Orleans if you want to. I don't care."

She climbed out of the ring, and headed for the change rooms.

I stared at the ceiling for a moment. That went well.

I sat up. I wasn't done.

13

BELL

I slammed into the women's change room.

Thank God, it was empty.

"*Argh.*" I paced by the lockers. How dare Beau touch me? With hands he'd put on another woman last night.

I didn't sleep with her.

It wasn't any of my business, but knowing he hadn't slept with the gorgeous, perfect Klara made my belly quiver.

I whirled again. I couldn't let myself have feelings for him. I couldn't afford it.

And I couldn't afford to put Beau in the firing line. I swallowed. If Carr knew Beau was close to me, I'd be painting a target on Beau's back.

I yanked my backpack out of my locker and opened it.

I saw the notes from Carr, and my stomach curdled.

They always stayed in my backpack. A bad taste filled my mouth. They were a reminder that I couldn't get close to anyone, that I had to survive.

The door to the change room slammed open. I spun and my mouth dropped open.

Beau strode in, looking like some dark god of the underworld. Like a man on a mission.

"This is ladies only," I snapped.

"It's my gym."

He kept coming. I backed up until my back hit the lockers.

He stopped just a few inches away, and pressed his hands to the locker over my head.

"What are you doing?" I asked.

"I wanted to clear the air. I want you to fucking look at me."

I gritted my teeth and met his gaze.

He frowned. "You afraid of me?"

Now, I frowned. "No."

The lines on his forehead eased. "Good." Then his fingers brushed my hair. "Bell—"

"I can't do this." I ducked under his arm. "Go back to your brunette."

He turned. "The date sucked."

I felt a spurt of pleasure. "I'm sorry to hear that." *Lies. All lies.*

"It sucked because I was thinking of you," he murmured.

Warmth spread through me, and I dragged in a shaky breath.

"I didn't want to be with her. I was thinking of pretty, blue eyes."

"Beau—"

"I know. You're too young, and too damn good for me."

Too good? The man was...everything I wasn't. He was successful, settled, knew who he was.

"I hurt you," he murmured.

I bit my lip and looked away. "No, you didn't."

He stepped closer. "Don't lie to me. I saw your face when you first saw Klara. Damn, I hated seeing that look on your face." He took another step.

Paper crinkled.

I looked down. He'd stepped on one of the notes.

Oh no. Horror filled me.

"That's mine." I lunged down to snatch it up.

But Beau beat me to it and picked it up. He opened it. As he read it, I saw his face harden.

"What the fuck?" he whispered.

I snatched the note out of his hand and turned to my backpack. "Forget you saw that."

"It's fucking impossible to forget that filth." He shouldered past me. He saw the other notes in my backpack and pulled them out.

"Beau, no." I grabbed at his hand.

He held the notes above my head and started reading another one. A muscle ticked in his jaw.

I knew what he was reading. Every sick detail of what Chandler Carr wanted to do to me.

The horrible things he'd done to Allison.

"Give them back," I whispered hotly.

He kept holding the notes over my head.

I saw the rage building on Beau's face.

"Who is this fucker?"

"No one. This is none of your business."

His anger intensified. "The sick fuck... He wants to kill you."

"Trust me, Beau. Take the statuesque brunette out again. Stick with Klara. She's easy, with no baggage." I pulled the notes from his fingers. "This is my shit to deal with."

His jaw worked. "You're in danger."

Then he spun, and slammed a big fist into one of the lockers. The metal dented.

I gasped.

He punched it again.

The violence, the power, all of it fueled by anger on my behalf.

He whirled, his mouth a flat line. "I don't fucking want Klara. End of discussion. And you are *not* dealing with this alone."

I couldn't move. I swallowed, too many emotions building up inside me.

Beau leaned in. "This is my fucking business. I'm making you my business. So get ready."

Then he turned and stalked out.

I stared after him. *What the hell had just happened?*

I wasn't exactly sure, but something had, and I figured I'd better get ready to deal with it.

14

BEAU

I carried the box off the truck and into the warehouse.

My mind was still churning. Still running over those vile, sick notes in my head.

I set the box down with some others stacked by the wall, then skirted Kav and Reath carrying other ones, and strode back to the truck.

We were dropping off donations to a local charity that supported foster kids. The boxes were full of kids' clothes, school supplies, toys and games, and toiletries. I yanked another box off the truck.

When I turned, all four of my brothers were standing in a row in front of me.

Colt crossed his arms over his chest. "What's going on with you?"

I frowned. "Nothing."

"Beau, you've been like a damn robot since we picked you up this afternoon," Reath said.

"I'm fine."

"A grumpy robot," Kav added. "We can all sense the storm gathering. You'll explode soon."

I released a breath. They were all nosy as hell, and would never leave anything alone.

"It's the young woman working at his gym," Dante said. "Bellamy."

My muscles tensed.

"Ding, ding," Reath said. "Dante wins the prize. So, what's going on?"

"Did she turn you down?" Kav asked.

I set the box down at my feet, then raked a hand through my hair. "No."

"You are her boss," Colt said.

All my brothers turned to look at him.

"Macy was your office manager when you fell for her," Reath said.

"Office *assistant*," Colt corrected.

Kav, Dante, and Reath all snorted.

"And Mila worked for Dante," Kav added. "Workplace romances are bit of a thing around here."

"I've already fucked her," I said. "A month ago."

My brothers all went silent.

Dante scratched his jaw. "Spill."

"It was when I was driving back from Texas. I pulled into a motel near the border. It just happened."

"Okay," Dante said slowly.

"She snuck out. I never knew her full name."

"Ouch," Kav said.

I rubbed my forehead. "She ended up at Hard Burn this week, wanting to learn to fight. She had no idea I owned the place."

"Are you sure?" Reath said.

I scowled at him. "Yes, I'm sure. She's not playing some game, here. She's on the run. My first guess was she was running from a bad family life, but it's worse than that." I shook my head. "I read these notes she has... Some sick fuck is after her. God, what he wrote, what he says he wants to do to her." I shook my head.

My brothers all sharpened. Growing up in foster care, none of us had a minute for anyone who preyed on those who were weaker and vulnerable.

"Who is he?" Reath asked.

"I don't know. She won't talk. She's all bottled up and wrapped in fierce independence."

"Ah, independent women," Kav said. "Irresistible."

"And she's afraid. She's been running and alone for who knows how long."

"Is she safe?" Reath asked.

"As far as I know, this fucker doesn't even know she's in New Orleans. Bellamy's not her real name, and she's staying at some boarding house near the Garden District. She's living under the radar so whoever he is, he can't find her."

"Want me to look into her?" Reath asked.

"No." I blew out a breath. "I want her to tell me. I want her to trust me."

Dante raised a brow. "That's a first."

"Dammit, I can't stop thinking about her. Not just about the sex. I want to...look after her. Keep her safe."

"Claim her as yours," Dante murmured.

My mouth twisted. "I can't. She's too young—"

"She's an adult, Beau," Reath said. "And she's dealing with some heavy shit."

I scraped a hand through my hair. "It's not just her age. She's...got this innocence to her. I don't deserve to touch her."

Now, my brothers all looked pissed off.

"*Bullshit*," Reath said. "You're a fucking good guy."

"I'm big, tough, tattooed. And I come from scum."

"That's fucking bullshit," Dante said. "You're the man you've made yourself to be. None of us are who birthed us. My parents were no angels."

"Mine abandoned me in a box at birth," Reath said.

"Yeah, well none of them tried to sell you to score their next fix." The words came out of me like poison. "That's what I come from."

Reath grabbed the front of my shirt. "No, you're Beauden Fury. The man who joined the Army with me to keep me safe. The man who taught me how to protect myself."

"A good man, a good brother," Colt said.

"Who's always had our backs," Kav added.

Dante nodded his head toward the box at my feet. "Who just delivered boxes of things for kids in need."

"That's who you are," Colt said.

"You've got feelings for Bellamy," Kav said. "You need to work them out."

"Either claim her as yours, or set her free," Dante said. "Help her find a place where she'll be safe."

The idea of Bell leaving, of being far away from me, felt like claws digging into my gut.

Kav grinned. "I think you already know the answer."

Fuck, yeah.

Bellamy was mine.

Or at least, she was right now, while she needed me.

Now, I just needed her to realize it.

15

BELL

I t had been a busy day.

Gio had wanted some deep cleaning done, so he'd put me to work. He had let me work out in the gym during my lunch break. The guy acted tough but was a marshmallow inside.

I'd only had a few glimpses of Beau. I bit my lip. I'd kept waiting for him to say or do something all day.

I hated that he'd seen the notes.

I wiped down some equipment. The women's self-defense class had just finished up, and Shay had just left. Karina had stopped by earlier for a quick workout and brought me cookies she'd made from carrots. They'd been disgusting, but I'd choked one down. She was so nice, and I didn't want to upset her.

The gym was closing soon. The rings were almost empty, and I spotted Beau talking with one of the boxers on the far side of the gym.

"Girly, I'm going home." Gio pulled a light wind-breaker on.

"Okay, Gio. Night."

He eyed me for a long moment, then nodded. "See you tomorrow."

I smiled. I liked the crusty, old guy.

I moved to the reception desk, and tidied up the surface. The door opened as someone entered.

"We're just about to close." I looked up.

Oh, God. My stomach dropped. It was the beautiful brunette, Klara. God, had Beau made another date with her?

Was all the stuff he'd said to me bullshit?

"Um, hi. I'm not here to work out." Klara fiddled with her hair. "Is Beauden available?"

I forced myself to act like a human. I swallowed the lump in my throat. "Let me check." I swiveled. I really didn't want to look at her perfect face and perfect hair.

I headed back into the main part of the gym. I saw Beau and he smiled at me. Then he saw my face.

"What's wrong?" He gripped my arms. "Did you get another note?"

I shook my head. "Someone's here to see you."

He looked over at reception, and his face evened out. He blew out a breath.

"Another hot date?" My tone was sharp.

His fingers squeezed my arm. "Bell, one thing I'm not is a liar." He shook his head. "I *should* go out with her. She's close to my age."

"And beautiful and accomplished. And like I said before, she probably has no baggage." Even I heard the misery in my voice.

Beau touched my jaw. "I'll talk to her, then it's

training time. Go and get ready." He let me go and stalked off.

I didn't stay to watch them. I needed to train.

Carr would eventually find me, and I had to be ready.

After getting changed, I headed for our training ring and got busy putting my wrappings on.

A little while later, Beau appeared. "I've locked up, so we'll have no interruptions."

I glanced at the front door and saw the lights were off. "She's gone?"

"Yes."

I shifted on my feet. "Why did she come?"

He sighed. "To see if we could salvage things. I told her no." He picked up the focus pads. "Now, let's train."

I climbed into the ring. I knew we wouldn't be visible from the front windows.

With just the nearby light on low, it felt like it was just the two of us—like no one else existed.

He held the pads up. "Let's see what you've got."

I hit the pads, warming up. After a few combos of hits, my muscles felt warm and fluid.

"You really don't want to go out with her?" Shit, I hadn't meant to say that.

His stormy gaze hit mine. "No. I don't want her."

I bit my lip and nodded.

"No distractions," he said, waving the pads. "Now, get back to work."

I rammed punches into the pads, circling around Beau. He barked out commands at me.

"Wait." He paused and touched my elbow. "Keep this strong. You need the power."

I nodded.

We kept going, and I lost myself in the fight. Well, not completely. I was conscious of Beau—his big body and tattoos, his commanding presence.

He lowered the pads and nodded. "Good work. Let's call it a night."

My muscles felt like jelly, and my tank top was soaked with perspiration. "I can go longer."

"That's enough for tonight. You don't want an injury." He pulled a pad off one hand, and touched my shoulder. "You're a fast learner, and doing well."

Pleasure washed through me and I nodded. I slipped through the ropes.

"You ready to tell me about him? The man hunting you?"

I froze, my muscles going tight. I stayed silent.

Carr was my horror. If I talked about him... It felt like I'd summon him, or something. I knew it was silly, but it was hard to shake.

Right then, all I felt was a tight ball of fear and pain in my chest.

Behind me, Beau sighed. "Go and shower."

I didn't linger long under the hot water. It was late, and I figured Beau wanted to get home. When I walked back into the gym, there was no sign of him.

"Beau?" With only a few low lights on, there were so many shadows in the gym. "Beau?"

A force hit me from behind. I went down on the training mats with an *oof*. I was pinned.

Fear was like a spike in my chest. I started jerking.

"You need to know how to break the hold of someone

bigger and stronger than you." Beau's deep voice in my ear. His warm breath brushed over my skin.

I relaxed, even as my heart hammered. It was just Beau.

"No, don't relax. Think. This fucker, he won't come at you from the front. He won't fight fair."

Beau was right.

I bucked and tried to shift my weight, but he was too big and strong.

"Reach back," he said. "Poke him in the eyes, pull his hair."

I obeyed and grabbed Beau's thick hair, and pulled. He grunted.

I managed to get a foot up under me, and pushed. It gave me enough leverage to unbalance him.

I slithered out from under him, scrambled, and rolled.

But a second later, he was on me again.

This time, he pinned me down on my back. We were face-to-face. My heartbeat picked up for a different reason.

"Now what?" he asked.

I decided I needed the element of surprise. I raised my head and kissed him.

As my lips moved over his, his big body went slack.

I hadn't kissed anyone in a really long time. Kissing Beau felt good.

That's when I rammed an elbow into his side. He reared up enough that I wriggled free.

In a crouch, I grinned at him.

"Clever," he said. "But you *never* use that move on anyone else."

"I won."

His gaze moved over my face. "I thought you didn't do kissing?"

I swallowed. "I haven't for a long time." I paused. "I haven't wanted to kiss anyone."

"But you want to kiss me."

Everything inside me tingled and melted. "Beau—"

Then he lunged.

I screamed and sprung. I tried to crawl across the mats.

He trapped me on the mat on my belly.

"Now what?" he murmured.

I swallowed. "I'm not sure I want to get away."

"*Bell.*" My name was a low groan. He pressed his face to the back of my neck.

Then I felt his hands pushing my shirt up. His beard and lips moved along my spine.

I gasped. I felt a rush of damp between my legs.

He growled, nuzzling lower. "I can smell your arousal."

"*Beau.*" It was a whimper, a plea.

Before I knew what was happening, he was pulling my leggings down, baring my ass.

"Look at you." His voice was all grit. "Beautiful."

Rough fingers delved between my legs. I moaned, and lifted my hips to give him better access. He stroked me, igniting fires everywhere.

"Got to eat your pussy, angel. That taste, it's all I've thought about for a month."

I made a sound, then he gripped my buttocks, and buried his face between my legs.

With a cry, I rocked forward. He licked me, his tongue doing things that made me bite my lip. He licked, sucked, and tasted. His tongue parted me, and I wished I could sink my hands into his thick hair. Instead, I gripped the mat.

"You taste like a goddamn miracle," he breathed against me.

Then he went back to pleasuring me, eating me like a starving man. He paid attention to everything that made me gasp and writhe. Learning what I liked best, doing things I never even knew I liked. I chanted his name, and his tongue rubbed over me. He alternated between rough and gentle, licking and sucking until tears ran down my cheeks.

"Fuck, Bell. So sweet." He closed his mouth over my clit.

I exploded. My orgasm hit so hard I couldn't think, couldn't do anything but cry out his name. Sweet relief felt like pure heat washing through me, stealing the air in my lungs, making my muscles go lax.

Eventually, I flopped onto the mat, panting.

He pressed a kiss to the top of my ass. "Better than I remembered."

I couldn't think, I could barely breathe. I was just a melted puddle of pleasure.

Then he reached around and touched my cheek, my lips. "Come on. I'll drop you home."

16

BEAU

Pulling my Rivian EV truck over to the curb, I scowled at the old mansion on the edge of the Garden District.

The two-story building had probably been graceful and elegant once, now it just looked old and run-down. Emphasis on old.

"There are only women staying here?"

Bell turned in the passenger seat to face me. "Yes. And the front door stays locked at night, and every room has a lock."

I grunted. I still didn't like it. I'd prefer she stay somewhere with top-notch security.

"So, I'll see you tomorrow." She fidgeted a little in her seat.

I wondered if she still felt my mouth and beard between her legs. If she was sensitive and swollen. Damn, she'd tasted so good, and I'd loved every sound she'd made. I knew I shouldn't have touched her, but the desire had just been too strong. I was already hungry for more, my cock still half hard and begging for release.

"You'll see me tomorrow. Bell, if anything worries you, you call me."

She smiled. "I will."

My gaze dropped to her mouth. She'd kissed me earlier. Yes, it had been a tactic to escape my hold, but she'd pressed her sweet mouth to mine. And I knew kissing was hard for her.

That it meant something.

"Beau?"

I flicked my gaze up to hers. "You kissed me earlier, but I barely got a taste of you."

Even in the dim light, I saw color fill her cheeks. "I'm pretty sure you got a really good taste of me in the gym."

I made a low sound and grabbed her hand. It was so delicate with slim fingers. "I did. And I loved every second of licking you."

She pulled in an unsteady breath.

"But I want to taste your mouth as well. Will you let me, Bell?"

She was silent for a moment, her gaze tracing my face. I liked that she was thinking it over so hard. That she didn't just kiss anyone.

Then she nodded.

I pulled her closer and leaned over the center console, resenting that it was between us. With my other hand, I cupped her face.

Her eyelids fluttered but she kept her eyes open, her blue gaze locked on me. Then I brushed my lips over hers.

She let out a soft sigh and I licked the seam of her lips. She opened for me, her hand coming up to press against my cheek. I kissed her how I'd wanted to that night in the motel, with both of us wet from the rain and hungry for each other.

She made a sexy, little sound, and I kissed her deeper, our tongues tangling. It was perfect. No awkward hesitation or wrong moves. It was like we'd kissed each other a thousand times.

This time it was me who groaned. Damn, she tasted like the sweetest drug, and I wanted more. I barely resisted hauling her across the console and onto my lap. When she kissed me harder, demanding more, I held onto my control by a thread.

Bell was vulnerable and young, and I never, ever wanted her to feel pressured into anything that happened between us.

Her nails scraped against my beard, and I took more of that sweet mouth. Devoured her. My cock was a hard, pulsing ache between my legs.

When I lifted my head, she was panting and looked dazed.

"Why did you stop?" she whispered.

"Because it's time for you to go inside, angel." I fisted my hand in her hair and dragged my mouth over hers one last time.

She licked her swollen lips. "Okay."

"Good." I smoothed her hair back. "I'll see you tomorrow."

With a nod, she grabbed her backpack, then climbed out. I watched her jog up the sidewalk, then through the gate, and up to the front door. She gave me a wave and disappeared inside.

I didn't start the truck or drive off. I sat there in the darkness and watched a light flick on upstairs.

Bell was getting under my skin. I made a scoffing sound. Wrong, she was already burrowed in there.

It's just temporary. I wasn't built for anything long term. Right now, she needed help, and I wanted to help her. One day, when she was free of this situation, she'd move on.

I dragged my gaze off her window and scanned the street, searching for anything or anyone who shouldn't be there.

Everything seemed fine.

Wait. I saw something move by a tree down the street. I stared, trying to get a better look. Was someone hiding there? I glanced back at the house. Whoever it was would have a perfect view of Bell's boarding house.

I kept staring, and a moment later, a dog ran out. It sniffed its way down the sidewalk, pausing to cock its leg on a fence.

My shoulders relaxed. False alarm.

The light in Bell's room went off.

I started the truck, then headed for home.

Sweet dreams, angel.

———

I SET out the food on my desk as I waited for Bell to arrive.

I'd bought beignets—lots of them—from Macy's

favorite place. Colt's woman claimed they were the best in New Orleans. I'd also grabbed some egg-and-bacon rolls. Bell needed the protein.

I wanted to take care of her. Pausing, I stared at the wall, my jaw tight.

I'd gone through all the reasons I shouldn't touch her. Multiple times. Starting with the fact that she was too young for me, and too vulnerable.

Pressing my hands to the desk, I dragged in a breath. I'd vowed a long time ago that I'd never claim a woman as my own. Never marry. Never have kids.

I'd come from trash. Some things shouldn't be passed on.

And then I'd gone and stripped Bell half naked on the mats and gotten my mouth on her.

Right now, all I knew for sure was that I was keeping Bell safe from the sicko who was after her.

Whatever it took.

I checked my watch. She should be here soon.

I headed out into the gym and called out greetings to some of the regulars in the boxing rings.

Glancing out the windows at the front of the gym, I took in the gloomy New Orleans day. A brisk breeze was blowing, sending dried, fallen leaves swirling around on the street.

As I peered down the sidewalk, I spotted Bell.

She had her head down, a hoodie on, walking fast. I wondered if she ever relaxed, ever felt safe enough to let her guard down. She approached Hard Burn, hitching her backpack up on her shoulder.

Suddenly, a dark shape darted out from between two parked cars on the street and crashed into her.

What the fuck?

I sprinted to the front door and wrenched it open. Then I was racing down the sidewalk, pumping my arms.

The man in the black hoodie slammed Bell into the side of a car. Her backpack hit the ground. She was struggling with him, and got a good punch in.

"Hey! Let her go!" I roared.

The man's head jerked up. I got a glimpse of a pale face and a nasty grin, but then I realized his face was covered in some sort of weird clown mask.

He grabbed Bell and shoved her to the ground, then he turned and ran.

My hands curled into fists. I wanted to chase him.

The man darted across the street, dodging the cars. Several slammed on their brakes, tires screeching and horns honking.

Then he was out of sight.

Bell.

I focused on her, dropping to kneel beside her. "Bell. Fuck."

"I... I'm all right." She sat up. She had a small scrape on her face, as well as her palms.

"Was that the fucker?" I asked.

She swallowed. "I'm not sure. He was wearing a mask, and he didn't say anything."

This had to be related.

I helped her up and scanned the street. "Come on." I wanted her safe inside Hard Burn.

She took a few steps, wobbly as a fighter who'd just been sucker punched.

I scooped her into my arms.

"Beau—"

"Quiet."

Gio was holding the front door open for us, a fierce frown on his face. "You okay, girly?"

"She will be."

I carried her straight into my office, and kicked the door shut behind us.

"It's time you tell me who he is."

Big, blue eyes met mine. So much pain.

"I need to know so I can protect you," I told her.

"I can protect myself."

"By running?" I sat on the couch in the corner of my office, settling Bell on my lap. "You even think about running, I *will* find you. That is *not* an option."

I hated the thought of her disappearing and me being unable to find her.

"Beau..." She started shaking.

I smoothed her tangled hair back. "You're safe now."

"We both know I'm not. I can't believe he found me. Again." Despair in her voice.

I wondered just how many times this guy had found her, scared her.

The shaking got worse. "Sorry," she whispered.

"You have nothing to be sorry for. It's a normal reaction. What can I do to help?"

She swallowed. "I need a hug."

I wrapped my arms around her, and she buried her face in my neck.

"You're safe." I rested my chin on the top of her head. "You're going to be okay."

We sat there for a minute, just holding each other. Then there was a brief knock at the door.

Gio barged in, holding the gym's first aid kit. "For her hands." He set the kit on the desk, eyed us for a second, then left quietly.

Setting Bell on the couch, I leaned forward and opened the first aid kit. I tore open an antiseptic wipe. "Show me your hands."

"They aren't bad."

I just stared at her.

With a huff, she lifted her palms.

She was right, they weren't too bad, but I took my time cleaning her hands. Then I opened a fresh wipe and dabbed at the scrape on her face.

My thundering heartbeat was finally slowing down. She was safe. For now.

And I needed to keep her that way.

I needed to talk to Reath. He could help. But first, I needed details.

"It's time you talk to me, angel. Let me in." I took one of her hands in mine. "Let me help you."

She looked up and nodded. "Okay. I'll talk."

17

BELL

With Beau beside me, his strong hand holding mine, I felt a little steadier.

I dragged in a deep breath. I hated feeling weak and scared.

I wouldn't give Carr the satisfaction.

I glanced around Beau's office, and that's when I saw all the food on his desk. I frowned. "What's all this?"

"I bought breakfast for you."

I blinked, looking at the food. There was also a bottle of fresh orange juice. "Oh."

His callused fingers brushed my jaw, then he turned my face to his.

"Talk first, then you can try the best beignets in New Orleans. According to Colt's woman, Macy."

I imagined Beau didn't eat beignets often. I swallowed. "I don't know where to start." I twisted my hands together.

"Start at the beginning."

I nodded. "I met my best friend Allison, Allie, in the

second grade. She was so much fun. Friendly. Smiling. Loyal. She grew into a beautiful woman. Red hair, slim body. *Everyone* loved her."

Beau was silent, not asking questions about why I was starting by talking about my best friend.

"We went to college together." Pain sliced through me. "We left Dallas, that's where I'm originally from, and went to college at Baylor."

Beau tangled our fingers together. I realized my hand was shaking.

That small touch grounded me. I released a shaky breath. "We had so much fun those first years. I was studying business, and Allie wanted to be a nurse. She wanted to help people."

Misery wrapped around my insides, and I stared at the floor.

"Take your time," Beau said.

It was best to just get it all out. Taking my time made no difference to the grief and pain. "Allie had a date with a new guy she'd met at the campus coffee shop. Said he was so attentive and handsome." I rubbed my chest, a painful ache growing. "I was excited to have the night to myself. We shared an apartment. I ran a bubble bath, poured a glass of wine, put my earbuds in with my favorite playlist." I bit my lip. "I didn't hear anything. Nothing."

His fingers tightened on mine. "What happened?"

"Chandler William Carr happened." God, I hated that name so much.

Beau frowned. He'd probably heard the name and was trying to place it.

"Rapist and murderer. They call him the College Killer." Grief gripped me. "He raped and murdered Allie while I was in the next room taking a bath."

"Fuck."

"I didn't hear a thing, and she must have called for help," I whispered.

"It wasn't your fault, Bell." Beau's voice was a deep rumble. "*He's* the killer."

"I didn't hear a single thing while my best friend was hurt, dying. Do you know what that feels like?"

"No, angel, I don't." His grip stayed tight and firm on my hand.

"I came out of the bathroom and saw him leaving. He walked out of her room with a smile on his face, blood all over his hands. He erased Allie like she was nothing." My face twisted. "He's a monster."

"Why is he free?" Beau growled.

"I gave a statement to the police, and there was a manhunt. But he'd already disappeared. Allie was his fourth killing of a female college student across the South. His first in Texas." I dragged in a breath. "He's a college student from Georgia, raised by a good, well-off family who just happens to have a sick need to kill innocent women."

"I'm sorry, Bell. Sorry you lost your friend, that you had to go through that."

"My world turned into a nightmare. My best friend was dead, slaughtered." I paused. "Then it got worse."

Beau cursed under his breath, then pulled me back into his arms. I leaned into his strength.

"I couldn't stay in the apartment. I got my own place, but every day I grieved for Allie. It was hard to focus on my studies." I stopped, the old memories eating at me. "Then the notes started coming. He was watching me, and he knew where I lived. I'd see a glimpse of a shadow on the street after class. I'd find a note shoved under my door or under the wiper on my car. He was taunting me." I heaved in some air.

Beau's big hand rubbed up and down my back. "Take another breath. Remember, you're safe."

For the moment, I was, but as soon as I stepped back out onto the street, that was another story.

Carr had found me again. Despair swamped me. He never stopped.

"Carr attacked me when I was coming home from class one night. I tried to fight him, but I didn't really know how. Thankfully, I screamed loud enough for the neighbors to hear. He ran off." I sucked in air, trying to stay calm. "I was terrified. The police did what they could, but they couldn't track him down. I started training in self-defense."

"Good," Beau said.

"Then I got a nasty note, with a photo of my mother attached. Her eyes had been gouged out of the paper. The next day, a dead cat turned up on my doorstep, with its eyes gouged out." I looked up and met his gaze. I could feel the anger pumping from him. "I ran. To protect my mom, and myself."

"And you've been running ever since."

I nodded. "A year, now. I went to San Antonio, then Austin, a few smaller towns, then Houston. He always tracked me down. Then I made it to Pensacola. He found me again."

"The bruises on your arm."

I nodded. "I escaped him, just. Landed a good punch to the asshole's face." I sighed. "He just never stops. You've read the notes. He's fixated on me, and he wants to kill me."

"That's *not* happening." Beau's voice was a deep growl. "I'll teach you to fight, and we're going to stop this bastard."

"Beau, he's a killer."

"So am I."

My lips parted.

"I was in the Army, then I became a mercenary for several years." His gaze turned so serious. "Do you understand?"

I licked my lips. I wasn't sure that I did.

"Uncle Sam taught me to kill."

"Okay," I whispered.

He gripped my chin. "I would *never* hurt you or another innocent person. Chandler Fucking Carr picked the wrong city. This is *my* town. My brothers and I, we protect what's ours."

"I'm not yours."

"Yeah, you are. Now, tell me your real name."

I swallowed. Beau made it easy to let out all the secrets I'd kept locked up for a year.

"Isabella Sanderson."

"Isabella. It's pretty, but Bell suits you better."

I managed a small smile. "I like it better, too. Allie always called me Bell."

"For now, I want you to put Carr out of your mind. It's time for breakfast. Have you tried beignets before?"

"No."

"You're not a true New Orleanian until you've had one." He rose, and then handed me a sugar-covered pastry, followed by a glass of juice.

I took them from him. "You think this is going to solve my problems?"

"No, but it's a good place to start." He nudged the pastry toward my mouth. "I had a foster mom who told me having a full stomach is always the first step to solving any problem."

I took a bite of sugary goodness. Oh, God, that was delicious.

Smiling, he wiped the powdered sugar off my lips, then leaned down and kissed me.

My heart did a hard, one-two rap.

His lips moved over mine, but didn't linger. I hadn't really missed kissing, but with Beau, he made me want it. Badly.

"You're not alone anymore, Bell. Understand?"

I wanted to believe that. I knew exactly how much being alone sucked.

But Carr was beyond dangerous. What if he hurt Beau's friends or family? What if Beau got hurt?

The beignet turned to dust in my mouth.

A fierce look crossed Beau's rugged face. "You don't get it yet, but you will. Soon. Now, let's eat breakfast, then we'll work, then after that, we're going to take a break from everything."

"Where are we going?"

"Out for lunch."

Bell fiddled with her Hard Burn polo shirt. "Okay. I'm not really dressed to go out, though."

"This place doesn't require dressing up." I took her hand. I wanted to get her away. Out of the city, where there would be no fear that Chandler Carr would pop up and attack her. I led her to the back of the gym.

The first thing I'd done after Bell started work this morning—her belly full of breakfast— was look up Carr. My jaw tightened. What I'd read had made my skin crawl. He was a predator, through and through. He didn't just like to kill, he liked to torture and torment his victims.

Well, he might like to prey on helpless, young women, but now, he'd have to take on someone bigger and tougher.

"Bell." I gripped her shoulder.

She looked up at me, and damn, I saw the trust on her

face. I knew she'd been alone, with no one to lean on, for a year.

"I called my brother, Reath. He owns a security company."

She stiffened.

"I told him about Carr."

She pressed a palm to her cheek. "God, your brothers must hate that I brought this right to your doorstep."

"Hey." I turned her to face me. "They won't stand for an asshole like Carr murdering innocent women or terrorizing you. Reath's looking into him."

"Okay."

"We also have a friend in the New Orleans police department. He's going to do some digging. Simon's a detective, and he isn't real keen on a serial killer operating on his turf."

She nodded, her face uncertain. She didn't get that she was no longer alone in dealing with Carr. Now, she had the full force of the Fury Brothers on her side.

"Come on." I pushed open the door to my garage. Right now, I wanted her to forget for a while. Right now, there was no Carr. No fear or anxiety. I wanted Bell calm and relaxed.

"Oh, nice cars." She eyed my restored muscle car parked next to my black Rivian. She gently ran her fingers over the red hood of the car. "This is so cool."

"She's a 1969 Ford Boss 302 Mustang. I did all the work myself. Well, my brothers helped a little."

"It's great, Beau. It suits you." She smiled. "Are we going in this?"

"Nope." I skirted the car. "We're going on this." My Triumph Bonneville.

"Oh, I've never been on a motorcycle before."

There were some helmets hanging on the wall, and I grabbed one and handed it to her.

"That pink one's cute." She pointed to a small, pink helmet on the wall.

"For Daisy, my niece." I set the helmet on Bell's head and tightened the straps.

"One of your brothers has a daughter?" She tilted her head. "None of them looked like the typical dad."

I chuckled. "Colt. Daisy is technically his niece, but he adopted her."

Bell smiled. "I bet you all spoil her rotten."

"Guilty as charged." I turned and found a leather jacket that wouldn't absolutely swamp her. "Put this on. The weather's a little cool today."

As she did the jacket up, I pulled my own on. Then I threw my leg over the bike. I took a second to pull my own helmet on, then I patted the seat behind me.

She climbed on, settling on the leather. "I should have known you'd have a bike. It suits you too."

"Colt has a Harley. We ride together when we can." I pulled her arms around my waist. "Hold on tight."

She leaned into my back, and I felt a strange sensation.

Contentment.

I liked her there.

I started the engine and pressed the remote. The garage doors opened, and a second later, I rode out.

Bell clung tight as we drove to the Crescent City

Connection Bridge. As we crossed the river, I could tell she was looking all around, enjoying the view.

As I got off the expressway, taking some smaller roads as we headed south, the sun valiantly tried to make an appearance. I liked to ride. I liked the wind in my face, the road stretching out ahead of me. I rarely had a passenger, but having Bell with me added to the experience.

Finally, we went south through the city, heading toward the Jean Lafitte National Historical Park and Preserve. City gave way to wetlands and bayou.

We rode past a slow-moving creek, bounded by dense vegetation. After another mile, I turned onto a private driveway, slowing down as we wound through the trees. I pulled to a stop.

I helped Bell off the bike. She looked around.

"Where are we?"

"On the edge of one side of the Jean Lafitte National Historical Park and Preserve."

Her eyes widened. "Jean Lafitte the pirate?"

I smiled. "He was a complicated guy, and one of the most infamous characters in New Orleans history. He was a smuggler, a pirate, a spy, a folk hero. He did help fight off the British during the Battle of New Orleans. In return for a pardon for his crimes, of course."

She smiled back. "Of course."

"I like him. He did what he had to protect what was his." I shrugged. "I guess I enjoy the shades of grey." I held out my hand.

She took it.

"A friend owns this land." We reached the edge of the bayou. It was all dark, still water and cypress trees.

"Wow. It has a haunting sort of beauty."

I held her hand and led her to a wooden walkway. It ran along the water's edge and ended at a large, square platform over the water, circled by a railing.

In the center of the platform was a table with a white tablecloth, and plates covered by silver dishes.

Bell's mouth dropped open. "What is this?"

"Lunch." I held out a chair for her. "My friend who owns the land is also an exceptional chef. He owns a local restaurant on the bayou not far from here."

"You did this? For me?"

I nudged her into the chair. "For you." I sat across from her. "Out here, there are no bad guys or anything to worry about. There's only us, and maybe a few gators."

"Beau..." She pressed her hands to the tablecloth. "No one's ever done anything like this for me before."

That fucking broke my heart. I reached across the table and grabbed her hand. "You just need to relax, eat, and enjoy. Think you can do that?"

She nodded, her smile wide and happy. I realized that she didn't smile enough.

"Let's see what we have." I lifted the lid off the dishes.

"It smells great. I love crawfish."

"We have crawfish étouffée, chorizo jambalaya, and Cajun fried shrimp. All my friend's specialties." I served up the food, then poured us sparkling water from a cooler.

Bell ate with gusto, moaning, and asking for more. It gave me huge satisfaction watching her eat.

"This is so great, Beau." She looked out over the water.

"You deserve it."

She looked back, her smile fading. "Carr won't stop. I'll never be safe."

I growled. "You'll be safe when we stop him."

"The police have tried and failed."

I rubbed a finger through the condensation on my glass of water, wishing I could have five seconds in the ring with Chandler Carr. "I won't fail."

She looked stricken. "If he knows you're in my life, he could target you. He threatened my mom." She reached for my hand. "I don't want you hurt, Beau. I couldn't bear that."

"You're worried about me?" No one worried about me. I was a big, tough motherfucker.

"Yes." Her hand was so small and slender compared to mine.

"Don't worry, Bell. I'm not easy prey." I stroked her wrist. "I won't let him hurt you. I protect what's mine."

She stared at me. "You could have any woman you want. Like Klara. I'm...a mess."

I pushed my chair back, then reached over and lifted her out of her chair. I set her on my lap.

"You're strong, courageous. You grieve for your friend and protect your mom. You've sacrificed so much to survive. That's pretty fucking special to me."

19
———

BELL

This man.

    This gruff, rugged man was good, through and through. I knew how rare that was. How did I get so lucky to stumble into him, not once, but twice?

His mouth closed over mine, his beard tickling my skin. I heard the low rumble in his chest, and I bit his bottom lip.

"You're taking care of me," I whispered. "Spoiling me." I ran my hands over his shoulders, then shifted so I straddled him.

His gray eyes bored into mine. "I don't expect payback." His voice was gruff.

"I know." I nibbled his lips some more. "This isn't a thank you. It's just pure, old-fashioned desire." I opened my mouth and deepened the kiss. I slid my hands into his thick hair. "I want you, Beauden Fury."

With a growl, he took over the kiss. It got heated fast, and my fingers tangled in his hair. Everything slipped away: the fact that we were outside, the bayou, all my troubles.

It was just me and this man. Beau.

He sank a hand into my hair and tugged my head back. His mouth was on my neck, and he hit a sensitive spot. I moaned.

His hands pulled up my shirt, and he slipped it over my head. When he saw my pink lace bra, he gave a rumble of approval.

"Pretty." His fingers stroked my collarbones.

Then, he shoved the cups of my bra down, my breasts spilling free.

"Even prettier." His voice lowered an octave.

He hauled me up, and his hot mouth closed over one nipple. I cried out, and heard birds take flight from a nearby tree.

I couldn't stay still. As he nipped and licked at my nipple, I shifted, my ass rubbing on the cock I felt hardening beneath me.

He switched to my other breast.

"Tell me what you want." His teeth scraped my skin. "Tell me and I'll give it to you."

My chest hitched. I'd gone without everything for the last year. I hadn't gotten anything that I wanted. Being offered something was intoxicating.

"*You*," I whispered, undulating against his big, hard cock. "I want you, Beau. Your cock. I want your cock inside me."

He made a low, raw sound.

"*Please.*" I bit his lip. "Last night, on the mats after you made me come, all I wanted was to be filled by you."

"Stand up."

It was a gruff order. I obeyed, my legs feeling wobbly.

"Leggings off," he said.

I shoved them down. My pink lace panties matched my bra.

He reached down, and touched the side of them, flicking the elastic against my skin. Then his hand twisted, and he ripped my panties off.

I gasped.

"Now, you're even prettier." His fingers ran through the curls at the juncture of my thighs.

I stood there, naked for him, the breeze brushing over my skin. I shivered.

"Come here." His gray eyes were hooded.

My gaze dropped to the huge bulge in his trousers. I straddled him again.

"Mmm, I can smell how turned on you are." One of his hands stroked between my legs.

I was already saturated. I moved my hips, riding his hand. He was careful to tease, but not touch my clit.

"*Beau*," I pleaded.

He slid a thick finger inside me. "You don't get come to until you're full of my cock."

My womb clenched. I wanted that. *Badly*.

"Please, Beau."

He reached between us and opened his jeans. His cock sprang free.

Eagerly, I took it in both hands and stroked.

He groaned. "My greedy angel."

"*Hurry*. Inside me, now."

"Condom. In my wallet." His voice turned clipped.

I kept stroking him with one hand and fished in his pocket with my other. I pulled out his battered, leather wallet, then found the condom packet.

"Let me," I breathed. I ripped it open.

I rolled it on. His hips jerked, his cock pulsed to my touch.

"I can't wait any longer, angel."

I liked that he sounded as desperate as me. I pressed my hands to his shoulders and rose up. He notched his cock between my legs.

"Right there," he groaned.

I lowered down slowly.

Our gazes meshed, and we stared into each other's eyes. I slowly took him inside me, biting my lip as I felt the stretch. I'd forgotten how this felt. How big he was, and how well he filled me. Inch by inch, I pushed down until finally I had all of him deep.

"There it is. Balls-deep inside you." His hands gripped my hips. "Now, ride me."

I lifted my hips until just the head of his cock stayed inside me, then slammed back down. I kept moving, gaining speed and finding my pace.

It felt so good. Husky sounds escaped me, and I couldn't stop them. My fingers dug into his hard shoulders.

His hand stroked down my belly, and his thumb found my clit. He rubbed.

"God...." I gasped. "Yes, Beau."

"You like my cock inside you. Like me rubbing this slick, little clit."

His words had my belly tightening.

"I love the way you ride me, Bell. Taking me so deep."

I didn't last much longer. Two more plunges, and his thumb circling my clit, and I came.

I cried out his name as my climax hit. Pleasure rushed through me, my orgasm hotter and stronger than anything I'd ever given myself.

"Fuck, you're beautiful when you come."

I was still shaking when he slammed my hips down, lodged as deep as he could, and came inside me. His groan was long and loud.

Panting, I dropped my head against his shoulder.

He pressed a kiss to my neck. "My sexy Bell." His hand caressed my back.

Right then, I wished the real world didn't exist and I could stay right here forever.

20

BEAU

"Keep working on your uppercuts, Joey."

"Will do, Beau." My client wiped his sweaty face with a towel. We'd just finished a training session. "And thanks. I've really improved since I started training with you."

I nodded. "Happy to hear that."

Joey was in his mid-twenties and a keen boxer. He had a lot of potential. I watched as his gaze shifted, looking over at Bell. She was folding towels. I stiffened.

"Uh, your new hire, is she single?" Joey asked hopefully.

I frowned. "No."

My tone made Joey stiffen. "Right." He gave me a chin lift. "Got it. Night, Beau."

I watched him walk away. It was almost closing time, and the gym was emptying out. My cellphone rang and I pulled it out. Reath's name was on the screen.

I pressed it to my ear. "Hey."

"Hi, Beau. I've got an update on my search for Carr."

His serious tone made me tense.

"He's slippery," Reath said. "No credit cards in his name. No rental agreements, property, or cars. He's a ghost. But our facial recognition picked him up near the French Quarter."

My hand curled into a fist. I knew Reath's company, Phoenix Security Services, had invested a lot in cyber technology, including a state-of-the-art facial recognition system. "He's definitely in New Orleans, then."

"He is."

My knuckles turned white. "I won't let him get close to her again."

"I know. I've got my team hunting him, and I made a call to Simon. We'll find him, Beau."

"She needs new locks at her place. And an alarm she can press if there's trouble. I want to be the first one alerted." I pulled in a deep breath. I'd keep Bell safe.

"I'll have it taken care of."

"Thanks, Reath." I knew I could always trust my brothers.

Over the next few minutes, the last of the gym goers left, as did Gio. I locked the front door and turned the lights down.

"Everyone gone?" Bell smiled at me.

She looked relaxed. In my mind, I kept seeing her out on the bayou today, riding me in that chair.

My cock stirred.

"Yes. It's training time."

"I'm ready." She held up her already wrapped hands.

As we headed to the back boxing ring, I moved to the

music system and put some music on. The steady beat filled the air.

When I turned, Bell was in the ring. She'd taken her Hard Burn shirt off and was just wearing her leggings and a sports bra top. She bounced on her feet. "Come on, tough guy. I'm not afraid of you."

I liked seeing her smiling and playful.

I climbed in. "Don't get cocky."

She shifted from side to side. "I'm missing the appendage that usually leads to that. I think you're scared."

I wasn't scared of fighting her, but she did make me afraid of other things.

Of wanting to keep her longer than I should.

Of wanting more than I could have.

She came at me. I got my focus pads up just in time. Her hits made a solid connection.

We moved around the ring, doing all the combos I'd taught her. She moved well, and listened to instruction. She was a good fighter, and could read the cues.

"All right, drink break," I said.

She grabbed a water bottle from the edge of the ring and chugged it back.

"Let's make this more interesting." I dropped the pads to the mat and pulled on my own boxing gloves.

She cocked her head. "Okay."

"Let's have a little fight to test out what you've learned so far. Each point scored means the other has to pay up."

A groove appeared between her brows. "Money?"

I smiled. "No. A piece of clothing."

Her pretty mouth dropped open. "Strip boxing?"

"Now who's scared?"

"Not me." She whacked her gloves together. "I'm keen to see you naked, Fury."

I chuckled. "Let's go then, angel, because you're the one who's going to end up naked."

She came at me, and this time she was putting everything into it.

But I had the advantage of experience and longer arms. And I wasn't above using either of them to my advantage. I scored a light punch and Bell huffed out a breath.

She toed off one shoe, and kicked it to the side of the ring. "Don't go easy on me."

"No plans to."

We kept fighting. I lunged forward, and she dodged my swing nimbly, then planted her glove in my gut.

"Good girl." I yanked my T-shirt off.

Her gaze ran over my chest and my ink in blatant appreciation.

"Don't get distracted," I warned. "It's the first rule of fighting."

Her chin lifted. She attacked.

As the fight progressed, I lost a shoe, while Bell lost her other shoe, both socks, and then had to shed her leggings.

She stood in the center of the ring in her sports bra and panties.

My smile was slow and cunning.

"It's not over yet," she said.

I gestured with my gloves.

She moved faster, her hits riskier this time. We moved around the ring, and I avoided her swings easily. I could see the frustration in her face.

But she wasn't giving up.

Then, I lunged forward, my gloves hitting her side in a one-two hit.

"Dammit," she grumbled.

A second later, she stood in the center of the ring naked.

I loved her body—her fit build, her curvy breasts. "Looks like I win."

"Enjoy the moment."

My gaze ran down her body. "Oh, I will."

I hadn't had a chance to appreciate her that first time in that dark motel room. Nor the second time by the bayou.

Now, I could.

She met my gaze and licked her lips. "What now?"

Now, I took what was mine.

21

BELL

I could barely stop shaking. Desire was eating me up inside.

I wanted him.

I wanted Beau.

He drank me in and the look on his face told me how much he desired me. He made me feel strong, feminine, wanted.

Things I'd been missing for so long.

He yanked off his gloves and wraps, and reached out and cupped my breasts.

I gasped. Sensation shot from my breasts, straight down my body to between my legs.

"Now, I'm going to make you scream my name," he murmured. "Now, I want to make you come so hard, you won't remember your name."

God. My knees went weak. I loved the blunt talk. I pulled my own gloves off.

He dragged me down to the mat.

"I wanted to fuck you here last night." His voice was low and sexy.

"I wanted that, too," I whispered.

He kissed me, tongue plunging into my mouth, demanding and hot. It felt like a claiming. He pushed me flat on my back, then his hands were all over me, rough and firm. He caressed my breasts, plucking at my nipples.

"I love these pretty breasts," he murmured.

My nipples were so hard they were almost painful. The most pleasurable pain. I moaned.

"Touch yourself, angel. Get yourself ready to take my cock."

For a second, I hesitated, but the desire in his eyes urged me on. I slid my hand down my belly, and between my thighs. My lips parted, and I stroked myself how I liked. I was already so wet.

And the way Beau watched me made it even hotter.

"Fuck, yeah." His mouth was back on mine. He growled, his tongue sliding between my lips.

Yes. I slid my free arm around his neck. I whimpered into his kiss.

"Keep stroking that slick pussy, angel."

The sensations between my legs and in my belly were electric. Then one of his hands joined mine and I jolted.

Together, we stroked me, circling my clit. Then as I rubbed that swollen nub, he pushed a thick finger inside me.

"*Beau.*"

His big body moved against mine. I felt his hard cock behind the cotton of his shorts. Then he pulled away.

No.

He rose and shoved his shorts down.

Oh, yes.

His cock was big and swollen. I couldn't believe that I'd had that inside me.

He pulled a condom out of the pocket of his shorts, and I heard foil tearing. His moves were fast and jerky. Then he knelt between my legs. I watched as he rolled the latex over his thick cock.

My belly clenched. It was so sexy to watch.

Then he stroked his cock. "I can't wait any longer." He leaned forward, rubbing his cock between my legs. "I need to be inside you."

"Yes. Please, Beau."

He thrust forward, pressing his hands to the mats beside me. He filled every part of me.

I moaned his name, my eyes closing.

"Keep your eyes on me, Bell."

I snapped them open.

He started thrusting. We were connected, and it felt so good. Just the two of us. Beau and Bell.

His thrusts were slow at first. He slid deep, filling me with every inch.

"God, it's like you were made for me." His voice was deep.

My belly clenched hard. My hands dug into his thick shoulders. "I love you inside me. Taking me."

He made a low sound. "Need to fuck you now. You're too damn sweet, tight, and wet."

"Take me."

His hips thrust faster, and I gasped.

"Hold on, Bell."

I gripped him harder, my nails digging into his skin.

Then Beau fucked me.

His powerful thrusts moved me on the mats. With each heavy plunge, he bottomed out, and the base of his cock hit my sensitive clit.

My body shuddered with each thrust, and I felt my orgasm crashing closer.

"Beau!"

"Let it come, angel."

I gripped him and started coming. The pleasure was hot and fierce. I whimpered.

"Damn, you're so beautiful when you come," he gritted out.

He kept powering deep. I saw him glance down, watching as my body took him.

With his next thrust, his cock filled me, his hips pumping forward. I watched his muscles strain as he let out a low roar and came.

His climax took a while, and I couldn't take my eyes off him. So big and beautiful.

Finally, he sagged against me, rolling to the side so he didn't crush me.

I felt him playing with my hair. *Mmm.* I felt so good. Relaxed, pleasured, safe.

"We're going to need to disinfect this mat," I murmured.

He let out a low rumble of a laugh. "Yeah." He pressed a kiss to the side of my neck.

I let out a happy sigh, my eyes closing.

"No. We're not sleeping in a damn boxing ring." He scooped me up, and carried me out of the ring.

"Beau, we're naked! We need to clean up, and pick up our clothes—"

"We'll do it in the morning before opening."

He paused, and it took me a second to realize he was dumping the condom in the bin.

"Right now, I want you in my bed."

Oh. He carried me up the stairs. I was so curious about his apartment.

When he stepped into a large open space, I looked around. The place had a masculine vibe. The floor was wood, and the kitchen had dark cabinets. Cool, metal lights hung over a large, leather couch that faced a massive television.

The place was totally Beau. I saw a framed picture of him on the wall wearing his boxing gear, gloves held up in a fighting stance.

"That photo should be in the gym."

He grunted. "I'm not a poser."

He carried me up a set of stylish, open, wooden stairs to a mezzanine level.

It was ringed with a metal railing on one side. A big bed sat in front of some triangular windows under the eaves. It was covered by a dark-gray comforter.

He set me on the bed.

Then he rose and nodded. I saw satisfaction on his face.

"I like you right there," he said.

Warmth filled my chest. I liked it, too.

I held out a hand. "Come join me."

"Ready to sleep?"

"No." I got onto my knees. "I'm ready to suck your cock."

"Damn, Bell." I watched his cock jerk. "I shouldn't get hard again so soon after the way I came downstairs."

I bit my bottom lip. "I can get you hard again." I watched the way his gaze zeroed in on my lips. "I've been dreaming about sucking you."

Without hesitation, Beau climbed on the bed.

22

BELL

It was Saturday and the gym was full of noise. The chatter of excited kids and laughter echoed all around.

I smiled. Hard Burn was full of foster kids learning the basics of self-defense.

"All right." Beau's deep voice cut across the noise. "Let's try those moves again."

The eager kids got right into it. Some were boisterous, others quieter and more withdrawn. All the Fury brothers, along with Shay, Gio, and a few of Beau's other trainers, were helping out. I watched Dante get down to eye level with a shy girl and coax a smile out of her. A few minutes later, the little girl was trying the moves beside him. I bet Dante Fury could persuade any woman—young or old—to try a lot of things.

My gaze moved to Beau. He was so patient, with all his focus on the kids. They knew they had his full attention.

At the back, I helped a few kids who needed a hand, then headed for the kitchen.

It was full of the Fury women. They were currently making enough sandwiches and hot dogs to feed an army or two.

"I can't believe Kav bought a whiskey distillery," the bubbly blonde, Macy, was saying.

We'd had quick introductions when they'd first arrived, so I knew Macy was Colt's girlfriend, Mila belonged to Dante, and London was Kav's girlfriend.

"He said it'll be a good investment," the gorgeous London with dark skin and dark hair said.

"And best of all, I get to throw an awesome party there," Mila said.

London snorted. "You're always ready to throw a party."

Mila waggled her eyebrows. "And do it in style."

"Hi," I said from the doorway. "Do you need any help?"

The women all spun, holding knives covered in butter.

As they looked at me, I felt like a bug under a microscope. I fought the urge to shift uncomfortably. There was no way they could know that I was sleeping with Beau.

"Bell, right?" London said.

I nodded. "Right. And you're London."

She nodded.

"I'm Macy." The blonde wiped her hands on a kitchen towel and came toward me. She gripped my arm and dragged me into the kitchen.

I looked over at the brunette. "You're Mila. I saw your picture with Dante in the paper."

She smiled. "Guilty as charged."

"And I'm Daisy." A cute girl with her hair in crooked pigtails grinned at me. "Do you like pink, purple, red, or blue?"

"Um, all of them."

She beamed at me. "Me too." The little girl edged closer. "You work with Uncle Beau."

I nodded. "That's right. Here in the gym."

"Do you swear a lot?"

I blinked. "Oh, well, not really. Only when I'm really, really mad."

"Daisy has a swear jar," Macy explained.

"And Uncle Beau puts *lots* of money in it," Daisy added.

I laughed. "I bet he does."

"Where are you from, Bell?" London asked.

I fought back an uncomfortable feeling. I'd gotten used to not sharing my secrets. "Texas."

"Sorry I'm late." A woman with dark, tousled hair rushed in. "I got caught up in the lab and lost track of time." She paused and looked at me. "I don't think we've met. I'm Frankie."

"I'm Bell." I knew that Frankie was Reath's woman, and that they'd recently gotten together.

"Right." Frankie clicked her fingers together. "You're Beau's."

I blushed. "Oh, well...I'm his new hire."

Mila snorted. "We know you're sleeping together."

My mouth dropped open.

Frankie nodded and smiled. "The man watches you like you're a steak dinner."

Macy giggled. "And that man *loves* his steak."

I wasn't sure how I felt, being compared to meat. "Um..."

Macy touched my arm. "Colt told me that you're in trouble."

I froze, and my skin flushed hot.

Frankie's face was solemn. "Reath mentioned the man after you is really dangerous."

Now, I felt the color drain from my face.

"You don't have to talk about it, if you don't want to," Macy hurried on.

"God, you must think I'm horrible." I took a step back.

The women all look confused.

"Daisy, go out and help your dad and uncles," Macy said.

Daisy hesitated, and looked like she wanted to argue, but then the little girl ducked out of the kitchen.

"What do you mean?" Mila asked. "No one thinks you're horrible."

"You must think I'm horrible for bringing my troubles here," I said. "And dumping them on Beau."

The women all shared long looks.

"Here." Macy pulled a stool over. "Sit. Frankie, pour her some of the hot chocolate we made for the kids. London and Mila, you keep buttering that bread." Macy stepped in front of me. "No one can dump anything on Beau unless he wants it."

"Or any Fury brother," London added.

"Plus, Beau's a big guy," Frankie said. "Hard to dump anything on him that he can't handle."

"You don't understand," I whispered. "I have a serial killer after me."

"Pfft," Macy waved a hand. "I had a crazy stalker after me. Colt saved me."

Mila held up a knife. "I was hiding under a fake name while working at Ember. I was hiding from the killers who murdered my parents."

My heart squeezed. Mila's situation sounded similar to mine.

"I had an international criminal out for revenge after me." Frankie set a cup of hot chocolate down in front of me. "Plus, he wanted to steal my top-secret government project."

"Hey, I was next," London complained. "I had a crooked federal agent trying to frame me, and they kidnapped my sister."

"I win," Frankie said.

"No, I do," Mila shot back.

I looked at all of them. They were all smiling at me, welcoming me.

"The Fury brothers can handle a lot, Bell," Macy said. "Beau's holding a hand out to you. Take it."

I nodded, feeling overwhelmed.

She squeezed my shoulder. "These brothers, they've had their own rough time, and they all have their own demons. Just make sure that while Beau's looking out for you, you look out for him right back. Now, drink your hot chocolate."

23

BEAU

"**G**ood job, Ben. You've got a good punch on you."
The kid grinned at me.

God, I saw so much of myself and my brothers in this foster kid. From his ill-fitting clothes that he was growing out of, to his shaggy hair in need of a cut. I ruffled his hair and spotted a sullen kid standing at the edge of the mat.

I walked over. "Everything okay, Trey?"

The tall, lanky kid shifted on his dirty shoes. "Boxing is dumb."

I crouched. With his dark skin and dark eyes, he reminded me so much of a young version of Reath. "It's not for everyone, but learning to defend yourself is an important skill."

Trey hunched his shoulders. "Not if they're bigger and stronger than you."

My gut hardened, but I kept my feelings off my face. This kid had been someone's punching bag. I shoved the anger down. "There are ways to compensate if you're smaller."

ANNA HACKETT

The boy snorted. "You're huge. I bet you've never been small."

"I was once." A memory hit me—my mother screaming for me while a stranger, a man, stood beside her with hungry eyes. "And I was in foster care once like you."

Trey's lips pursed. "They said you were. You and your brothers." He glanced around. "No way those guys are really your brothers. I figured it was all lies."

"It's not lies." I pressed a quick touch to his arm, careful not to spook him. "We weren't born brothers, we chose to become brothers. We all went through foster care together." I paused. "How's your current home?"

Trey shrugged. "Decent enough."

"Good." I rose. "To be good at boxing, at any fighting, you need to use your brain first." I tapped his head. "It's about finding your advantages, and your opponent's weaknesses."

I could see him thinking.

"See that woman over there?" I pointed to Bell, who was setting a tray of sandwiches out on a table. "She's training to fight, and she isn't big."

Trey's face turned thoughtful. "She any good?"

"She's getting there. She's putting the training in. If you want something, you've got to put the effort in. You and I both know that life doesn't just give you the good stuff for free."

He nodded.

"How about you go and grab a hot dog?" I suggested.

This time Trey gave me a more vigorous nod. "Can I have two?"

I smiled. "Hell, yeah."

He shot me a small smile, then headed for the food table.

My gaze moved to Bell. She was smiling, and talking with the kids. I saw Macy stop and touch her arm. The pair chatted and smiled.

Good. My brothers' women were just what Bell needed. Another form of connection.

"Watching your girl again?" Colt asked.

I growled. "She's not a girl."

"Sorry, your woman."

Damn, I liked hearing that. "For now, she's mine, but it's temporary."

"Yeah, I tried that," Reath said. "Didn't work out." His gaze locked on Frankie. "Thank God."

"I mean it." My brothers stood around me. I looked back at Bell. "I'm glad you've all fallen in love, and I like your women. But I'm not interested in long-term, and I'm definitely never getting married. So, I'll help Bell out, and when she's safe, she'll go back to her life, and I'll go back to mine."

My brothers were silent.

"You deserve her, Beau," Dante said. "If she makes you happy."

"If you have feelings for her," Reath added.

I wish they'd just drop the subject. I felt a spike of anger. "Not happening. Now, let's get back to the kids."

"Beau." Dante gripped my arm. "Is this still about that shit to do with your parents?"

"It's about reality." I pulled free.

I heard Bell laugh and my head jerked up. Some young boys were pulling faces and making her giggle.

Yeah, I couldn't keep her, but for now, she was mine.

"THANKS FOR DROPPING ME HOME."

"I'm not letting you walk or take the streetcar now that we know Carr is in New Orleans." My Ford growled as I turned onto her street. I saw the boarding house and scowled. "You should've stayed at my place again tonight." I wanted her in my bed. That was new for me. I rarely had women back to my place, let alone staying overnight.

That was part of the reason I was dropping her home. I wanted her in my place too much. Maybe I needed a little space to remind myself that this thing between us wasn't a forever kind of thing. My brothers had all moved their women in when they were in trouble, and none of them had ever left. I couldn't risk that.

I pulled into a parking space on the street.

"Beau, you have late training sessions with two of your guys tonight. They have big competitions coming up. Then, you're up early to train with your brothers. I'd just be in your way."

I grabbed her wrist. "You're never in my way."

She smiled. "Besides, I need some sleep. Someone wore me out. And you know Reath's guys installed a heavy-duty lock on my door. It's so fancy that it looks like it's off the space station or something."

"And you've got that alarm?"

She held up the device. It was a panic button set into an elastic band around her wrist.

She leaned over the console and pressed a kiss to my lips. "Good night, good guy."

"Night, angel."

24

BELL

I woke up and rolled over, my single bed creaking. I instantly knew I was in my room at the boarding house.

I coughed.

Was that smoke?

My eyes widened, sleep dropping away. I reached over and flicked the lamp on, and it filled the room with weak light. But it was enough to illuminate the smoke creeping into the room like an evil spirit.

Oh, God. I leaped up. That's when I heard screams and running footsteps outside my door.

"Fire!" someone yelled.

My heart kicked into gear. Why weren't the smoke detectors blaring? I found my shoes and shoved my feet in, then yanked a hoodie over my pajamas. I had to get out.

I raced to the door and undid the fancy, new lock. Then I yanked.

The door didn't move.

What the hell? I yanked several more times, the door-knob rattling. I gritted my teeth and put all my strength into it. I yanked and yanked, but the door still wouldn't open.

"*Shit.*" Panting, I stepped back. Panic swelled in my chest and I swallowed. *Stay calm, Bell.*

I raced to the window. I gripped it and tugged.

It didn't open.

No. Despair licked at me. I glanced through the glass and saw flames engulfing the side of the wooden house.

Shit. Fear hit me like a fist.

I whirled. I had to find a way out.

I hammered on my door. "Help! I'm trapped, and my door is stuck. Please help."

There was no response. I heard people running and crying out. No one could hear me.

The smoke was getting worse, and I coughed some more. I crouched down where the air was clearer, and pressed the alarm button on my wrist. Then I fumbled for my cellphone.

Beau answered instantly.

"Bell?" Urgency underscored his voice. "Your alarm just went off. What's wrong?"

"*Beau.* God, Beau." I swallowed, then coughed. "Fire. There's a fire."

"What? *Fuck.*" I heard him moving around. "Get outside, but stay with the crowd. Carr could be using this to lure you out."

"Beau, I can't open my door. It's stuck."

He cursed. "The window?"

"It won't open, either."

"I'm coming, Bell."

"He did this." My hand clenched on the phone. "Carr is behind this. There are innocent people here and he set the house on fire. Others could still be trapped in here as well."

"I'm coming," Beau said. "Stay low. Put a wet towel over your head."

A sob escaped me.

"Bell?"

"I heard you." I lifted my chin. "I'm a survivor, Beau. I'll be here, waiting."

"Good girl."

The call ended, and I had to fight the crushing sense of aloneness.

Towel. I needed to wet a towel. I raced to my tiny bathroom, grabbed a towel off the rack, and put it under the faucet. Once it was wet, I wrung it out and wrapped it over my head. Then I found the corner of the room with the least amount of smoke, and sat down, pressing my knees to my chest.

Beau was coming. I just had to hold on.

25

BEAU

I drove as fast as I could toward Bell's place. The engine of the Mustang roared as I pushed for more speed.

Reath sat in the passenger seat beside me. Colt's truck was behind us, with Colt driving and Dante riding with him. Without hesitation, Dante had left his nightclub on their busiest night of the week. I'd called Kav, and he was on his way as well.

All I could think about was Bell. She was trapped in a burning building.

I stepped on the gas pedal, and took the next corner fast.

Reath braced himself. "Take it easy, Beau. Don't kill us."

"She doesn't have much time."

"You'll be more help to her alive."

I gritted my teeth and focused on the road. As we screeched onto Bell's street, I saw a crowd had gathered. I also saw the flames. My gut clenched.

I jerked to a stop near the burning building. Half of the house was engulfed. *Fuck.* My throat was tight. Bell was in there.

I shoved my door open and rushed toward the house.

Halfway up the path, Reath grabbed my arm. "No."

"I *have* to get to her."

My brother's face was set in grim lines. "Think first. You're no good to her hurt, or worse."

I forced myself to take a breath, fighting the urgent need to rush into the house. "I've got a leather jacket in my car."

Reath nodded. He was already wearing a black leather jacket.

I jogged back to the car and grabbed the brown jacket.

"Shit," Reath muttered.

I looked up and saw several women hanging out of windows on both stories of the house. They were all calling for help.

Bell's window was closed.

Colt's truck pulled up, and Dante and Colt jogged over.

"Fuck," Dante said.

"We have to help them," Reath said. "We need to get them out."

A sleek, red Lamborghini prowled down the street. Kav parked in the middle of the road and ran over. Right now, there was no sign of the billionaire businessman. Right now, he was just a man ready to help.

"Here." Kav handed out several masks.

I took one. "Bell's on the top floor. I'm going to get her."

My brothers nodded.

"I'll come with you," Kav said.

"Dante, Colt, and I will help the others out," Reath added.

In the distance, I heard the wail of sirens.

"Let's go," I barked, pulling the jacket on.

"Everyone away from the building," Reath bellowed at the crowd.

I charged in the front door. I wasn't waiting any longer.

I pulled my mask on. The smoke was intense. I ducked low, and headed for the stairs.

"This way," I heard Dante yell. When I glanced back, I saw him shepherding two women toward the front door.

I took the stairs two at a time. On the landing, I found a collapsed woman having a coughing fit.

"Kavner."

"I'll get her out." My brother crouched beside the woman. "I've got you. Come with me." He looked up at me. "Be careful."

With a nod, I kept going. The flames were intense at the top of the stairs, and I threw up an arm to shield my face. The fire was a lot worse up here.

I'd bet money that fucker Carr had set something alight up here.

I pulled the leather jacket up around my face and leaped through the flames.

"Bell!" I yelled.

I hurried down the hallway. Doors to the rooms

either side of the hall were open and empty. Then I heard a sob. I saw a woman crouched just inside the door to a bedroom.

"You need to get out," I said.

"I can't." There was terror on her face.

"You can." I slid an arm around her.

We'd just reached the top of the stairs when Kav charged through the fire. "Did you find Bell?"

"Not yet." I shoved the woman at him. "But I will."

Kav lifted the terrified woman into his arms, then carried her back down the stairs.

I strode to Bell's door. The smoke was thick as I hammered my fist on it. "Bell!"

At first, I didn't hear anything, and my heart squeezed hard.

"Bell!"

Then I heard a muffled noise on the other side of the door. "Beau!"

"Get back from the door." The handle was too hot to touch, so I used my jacket. But the door wouldn't move. I felt around.

Then I started coughing. The smoke was getting worse. My fingers ran over something.

Pure rage filled me.

The door had been nailed shut.

Carr.

I rammed my shoulder against the wood several times. Then I reared back several steps and kicked it. The wood splintered, but the door wouldn't budge.

Bending low, I went into the open room next door. I saw women's clothing spilled on the floor.

I needed something solid.

I spotted a chair with sturdy legs. I hefted it, testing its weight. It would do.

Holding it up, I ran back to Bell's door. I paused as a coughing fit overtook me.

Kav returned. "Beau, the fire's getting worse. The fire truck just pulled up."

"Bell's door is nailed shut."

"What the fuck?"

We didn't have time to talk. "Let's get it open." I picked up the chair. "Hold onto this. We'll use it as a ram."

Kav gripped the other side of the chair. We swung it back like a battering ram and stepped forward.

Thunk.

"Again," I yelled.

Thunk. Thunk.

Wood splintered and the door burst inward.

Thank fuck. Dropping the chair, I charged into the room.

"Bell! Bell!"

She crawled out of the smoke, her face streaked with black. "Here. I'm here."

I grabbed her. Relief was so strong that I felt dizzy.

"Rest of the rooms down the hall are empty," Kav said, followed by a cough. "Let's get the hell out of here."

Just as I'd told her, Bell had a wet towel wrapped around her. I tucked it more securely around her head and held her tight under my arm.

We hurried back down the hallway. Kav leaped through the growing flames and down the stairs.

I hunched over Bell, and followed.

The heat was immense, and I felt it on my cheeks. I kept my head down. The fire was getting worse, devouring the old house.

"Careful down the stairs." We took them slowly.

Suddenly, one of my boots went through one of the stair treads. I lurched to the side.

"*Beau.*" Bell gripped me.

Then Kav was there. He grabbed my arm. "The stairs are deteriorating. Move faster."

I yanked my foot free and kept Bell close as we reached the ground floor.

It was like Armageddon. Bell gasped. I couldn't hear it, but I felt her chest hitch.

Two firefighters in full gear approached from the front door. "You need to get out." One bellowed through his mask.

They shoved us forward.

"Anyone else in the building?" the second firefighter asked.

"I think it's clear," Kav said. "We helped get the last few residents out."

When we stepped into the cool night, I sucked in air and shoved my mask down. Bell thrust the towel off, lifting her soot-covered face up as she breathed.

She was alive. *Thank God.*

"That was close," Kav said, then he bent over, and coughed.

I slapped his shoulder. "Thanks."

He glanced at Bell, then back at me. "Anytime, you

know that. You've had my back too many times to count, and London's and her sister's."

I curled my arm around Bell as we crossed to the side-walk. Dante, Colt, and Reath were helping some women out on the curb. Some were crying, and the paramedics had oxygen masks on others.

"Anyone injured?" I asked Reath.

He shook his head. "Some smoke inhalation, but nothing life-threatening."

"Thank God," Bell said shakily.

"You need to get checked out," I told her.

She arched a brow. "So do you."

I was so damn glad to see that spirit of hers that I couldn't stop myself. I yanked her to my chest.

She made a sound of relief, and threw her arms around me. I boosted her up and she wrapped her legs around my waist. Then I kissed her.

It was deep and demanding, and I didn't care. I needed the reassurance.

"I was so afraid," I said against her lips.

"Me too, but I knew you'd come." She rubbed her nose against mine. "You and your brothers saved so many people."

My only thought had been her. I kept hugging her. We both smelled like sweat and smoke, but I felt her heart beating—strong and steady. And I tasted her on my lips—my sweet angel.

"You're next," a paramedic ordered.

"Her first."

A stubborn look crossed her face. "I'm only getting checked if he does."

I heard a chuckle nearby and saw my brothers. They all looked amused. *Assholes.*

Then I saw flashes of light. Dammit, the press was here. Just what we needed.

I pulled Bell closer and blocked her from view. Quite a crowd had gathered. I never understood the morbid need some people had to gawk at tragedies and accidents.

"God, all my stuff is gone." Bell looked stricken as the paramedic started checking her over. "What will I do? Where will I stay?"

That, I had an answer to. "We'll get you whatever you need." I cupped her cheek. "And you're staying with me."

Where I could protect her.

"Beau—"

"No arguments."

Her lips tilted up and she nodded. I leaned down and pressed a quick kiss to her lips.

Then she looked back at the house and the onlookers watching the fire. She stiffened.

"Bell?" I followed her gaze. She was staring at a man in the back of the crowd.

He had a clean-cut face and non-descript brown hair.

"It's Carr," she whispered.

The asshole smiled at us, then turned and disappeared into the crowd.

I tensed. "Kav," I barked. "Stay here with Bell." I looked at my brothers. Kavner nodded. "The rest of you, with me."

"What is it?" Reath asked, his face sharpening.

"Carr. He was in the crowd. Let's move."

I took off at a jog. As I cleared the crowd of onlookers, I caught sight of Carr sprinting down the street. He was wearing a pale-colored shirt and jeans.

"That way." I picked up speed.

Reath moved up beside me, and for a second, I remembered both of us in uniform, doing the same thing in a faraway desert. Colt and Dante ran behind us.

"You armed?" I asked.

"Yep," Reath replied.

Carr turned down the next street.

"Faster, or we'll lose him." My boots pounded on the concrete as I took the turn.

Carr looked back and saw us coming. He darted into the yard of a house. As I got closer, I saw him go over the side fence.

"I'll circle around the back." Colt headed back the way we'd come.

I hit the wooden fence and hauled myself over. Dante and Reath followed. I crept into the well-manicured back garden. There were neat garden beds, a garden shed, and an illuminated swimming pool. Then, I spotted Carr on the other side of the pool.

His gaze met mine. He looked so fucking ordinary. Then he smiled, and I could practically smell the evil.

He whirled and launched himself into some trees.

I took off, sprinting around the pool, and following the fucker.

"Hold up, Beau," Dante called out. "He could be armed."

There was no way I was slowing down. If I caught him, I could end this. Bell would finally be safe.

The asshole had locked her in a burning house. Rage fueled me.

I saw Carr clamber over a high hedge. I followed, feeling sticks claw at my clothes. Dropping to my feet on the other side, I saw Carr running down the street. Colt came sprinting from the other direction. Dante and Reath dropped down beside me.

"Don't let him get away," I growled.

All four of us took off, following the killer.

He crossed another street, then turned right. He was going into a school. In the darkness, I saw him racing across a soccer field.

I followed and pulled ahead of my brothers. I kept picturing the notes Carr had written, and Bell's face as she'd talked about her murdered friend.

Tonight, I was stopping him. Once and for all.

"You can't outrun us, Carr," I yelled. "You picked the wrong fucking city."

The man glanced back, and I saw him pump his arms faster. He sprinted past a building and back out onto the next street. This one was busier, with a grassed median down the middle.

Carr didn't pause, he raced across the street.

I wasn't letting him get away.

I went to step off the curb.

Arms gripped mine from behind and yanked me back. I stumbled and watched as a delivery truck whizzed past in front of me.

"Shit, Beau," Reath said.

He and Colt were gripping my arms. "Thanks."

Then I scanned the other side of the street. There was no sign of Carr. "Fuck!"

We crossed over and split into pairs. Reath and I jogged to the end of the block, while Colt and Dante did the same in the other direction.

"I don't see him," Reath muttered.

We walked back and met the other two. Dante shook his head.

We'd lost him.

Anger writhing inside me, I shoved my hands on my hips and stared into the darkness. The fucker was close, probably watching us.

If I'd caught him, this would have been over.

Colt clapped a hand on my shoulder. "We'll get him. Not tonight, but we'll get him."

"And we'll help you keep Bell safe," Reath said.

I nodded. I knew I could trust my brothers.

This isn't over, Carr.

26

BELL

I stepped into Beau's apartment, tired and reeking of smoke.

I had nothing. Carr had been chipping away at my life for over a year now, taking everything. Now, I had nothing left.

"Hey." Big hands settled gently on my shoulders. "Don't go wherever it is you just went."

His touch made me close my eyes and drag in a deep breath.

I wasn't alone. I nodded.

He took my hand and led me upstairs to his bedroom. "Take a shower. Wash the smoke off."

After we'd spotted Carr, Beau had mobilized. He'd left me with Kavner, while he, Reath, Dante, and Colt had disappeared into the night, hunting Carr.

They'd had no luck. He'd slipped away, and Beau had been mad.

Then, an unmarked police car had pulled up, and I'd gotten to meet Beau's cop friend, the sexy Detective

Simon Broussard. With his tousled hair and Cajun drawl, I guessed he probably never lacked for female company. He'd had a long conversation with the Fury brothers, and the firefighters.

I'd heard what they'd talked about. *Arson*. The smoke detectors had been tampered with, my door nailed shut, and they'd found accelerants on the second floor.

Carr had burned down the boarding house. *God*. In trying to get to me, he hadn't cared who else he hurt. I shoved my hair back off my face and realized that my hair reeked of smoke. My hands were streaked with soot.

"Shower, Bell," Beau said gruffly.

I managed a tired nod.

"Here, I got this for you." He handed me a T-shirt of his. It had Fury written on the back and I knew it was from his fighting days.

It was like he was marking me. I was an independent woman, so it wasn't supposed to make my belly quiver so much.

After a long look, Beau left, and I entered his small, but nice bathroom tucked under the eaves. It was all white tiles, with a few black accents. It also had a large walk-in shower.

As the water heated up, I stripped off my clothes. They were ruined. Great. It was a shame, because I'd liked the cute, green pajama set.

The hot water felt so good. I let it wash everything away.

But one thought remained.

Carr did this. He'd set the fire.

I knew he didn't want me to die in a fire. No, he had

grand plans for how he wanted to kill me—up close and personal. He'd set this fire for Beau. My stomach did an uncomfortable turn. Carr wanted to see if Beau would come, and maybe get hurt or worse in the fire.

My hands clenched. There was *no way* in hell that I was letting Chandler Carr hurt Beau.

Finally, I turned the water off and dried off. I pulled on Beau's T-shirt, and, unsurprisingly, it swamped me.

As I padded out of the bathroom, I heard music downstairs—a loud, angry rock song—and a rapid *slap, slap, slap*. I headed downstairs and saw him hitting a small speed bag that was attached to the wall in a frame.

His hands, just wrapped with no gloves, moved so fast they blurred. He was smacking the small bag hard.

He must've gone down to the gym to use the showers because his hair was damp. He was wearing a pair of black sport shorts, with no shirt. The muscles in his back were tense. My gaze traced over his tattoos—more of those fascinating geometric shapes and swirls. There were also some scars.

I bit my lip. Beau had lived a hard life, done tough things, and it showed on his body.

"Hi," I murmured

He kept hitting the bag, but glanced over. "Feel better?"

"A little. I don't smell like smoke, so that's a win."

I sat on the couch and the leather was cool on the bare skin of my legs. I curled up, careful not to flash Beau since I had no underwear on. I'd hand washed them, and they were hanging in the bathroom to dry.

All my lovely lingerie was gone. My perfume was

gone. My clothes were gone. Everything I'd owned had gone up in smoke.

I fiddled with the hem of my borrowed shirt. I was alive. No one had died. That's what mattered. I had to remind myself of that.

I focused on Beau. He kept hitting the bag, and it was mesmerizing to watch.

But I could see the tension, the contained energy in him.

"You're angry," I said.

"Yes. That we didn't catch him. That he fucking locked you up in a room in a burning house."

There was venom in his voice.

And more.

I rose. "It's not your fault, Beau."

"I left you there. I knew he was in the city. I shouldn't have let you out of my sight."

I touched Beau's back. "You left me with a secure lock and an alarm."

"He nailed your door shut," Beau bit out.

"I can't believe I slept through that, but the boarding house is never quiet."

"He set the fucking house on fire!" The words burst out of Beau like bullets. "I should have made you stay here. Where you were safe." He dropped his hands, and his breath hissed in and out of him through his clenched teeth.

"Beau." I leaned my cheek against his back. "You saved me. I'm alive because of you. No one's taken care of me for a really long time. I've only had myself to depend on." I paused. "It's nice not to be alone."

"Shit, Bell." He spun and cupped my jaw. "You're always breaking my heart."

"I might not have any clothes or my favorite perfume anymore, but Carr lost tonight. No one died in the fire. I'm alive and you weren't hurt. We won."

He nodded. "And now I have you right where I want you."

I smiled. "Is the big, bad boxer going to corrupt me?"

His face turned serious. "Some people would say I'm taking advantage of you. You're so young, less experienced, a woman in trouble..."

I laughed. "Most days I feel a hundred years old. Like I've seen way too much. The carefree college student, who worried about exams and dating and affording a new pair of sexy heels...I can barely remember what she was like. I'm a different woman now." I smoothed my hands up his chest, taking in the feel of his warm skin. I traced my finger over the lines of his tattoo, from one hard pec to the other. "A woman who is really happy she stepped into your gym."

"I'm glad you did, too."

I took his hand. "Do something for me?"

"Anything."

"Hold me."

27

BEAU

I'd changed the music to some low, slow jazz. Very New Orleans.

I was lying on my back on the couch with Bell snuggled in my arms. Her back was pressed into my chest, her fingers lazily stroking the tats on my arm.

My earlier tension had slowly drained away. Holding her eased the terrible anger and fury at Carr.

And at myself for not keeping her with me. Of being too much of a coward to take care of her properly.

Bell was right. She was alive. No one had been hurt in the fire. Dante had checked in with the owner of the boarding house, and the woman had insurance. Kavner had leaped into action and organized shelter for the women staying at the boarding house. They'd have a safe place to stay.

I played with Bell's damp hair. The dark strands smelled like my shampoo. It certainly smelled better on her than me. With her hair out, I realized just how long it was.

Her fingers moved over an old, raised scar on my arm. "Did you get this in the Army? Or when you were a mercenary?"

I released a slow breath. "No." I paused. "My mom stabbed me with a kitchen knife when I was five."

Bell's gasp was sharp. "What?"

I looked at the dark ceiling. I occasionally talked to my brothers about my childhood, but usually I gave my parents the least amount of mental time or energy as possible. "Both my parents had drug and alcohol addictions. They grew up poor and disadvantaged."

"That must've been hard on you."

"Yeah. Thankfully, there was just me." I'd had no other siblings who'd had to suffer. "Our house was chaos."

Bell pressed her face to my chest, offering quiet support. I held her close and felt as though a box cracked open inside me.

"The place was always stifling hot in the summer, and freezing in the winter. There was no money for heating or cooling. I went hungry a lot. I had to steal money out of their wallets. Then I'd roam the neighborhood." Anything to get out of the house. "They had people coming over to get high all the time. People coming to buy drugs."

"God," she whispered.

"If I got in their way, I usually got a slap." As I'd gotten older, the slaps had gotten more frequent and harder. "I turned into a big kid pretty quick, and I ate a lot. My parents resented any money they had to spend on me." They hated anything that might delay their next fix.

She made a choked sound.

"Shh. I survived, angel."

"*No* kid should have to survive that." She paused. "How did you end up in foster care? When your mom stabbed you?" Bell's voice sharpened. "I hope they locked her up."

So fierce. I smiled. "When child services checked in, she told them that I'd fallen on the knife. They believed her."

Bell cursed.

I stroked a hand down her side. "It was a few years later that I left." Chaotic images ran through my head— people, high on drugs, lying everywhere in the house, horrid smells, loud music. My parents strung out.

"I need it, Ray. I need a hit." My mother's stringent voice.

"He'll pay good money for the boy," my father said.

I carefully peered around the corner of the door. They didn't see me. I was good at not being seen.

My mother's brow creased. "To take him? Like, adopt him, or something?"

"No. For a few hours with him." My father wiped a hand across his mouth. "He promised he wouldn't leave any bruises."

My mother was silent and my rapidly beating heart had kicked in my chest. Was she finally going to defend me?

Then she licked her lips. "How much?"

I'd run. I'd already seen the way some of their friends looked at me. Especially one tall man whose dark gaze always followed me around. He gave me the creeps.

"My parents wanted to make money off me."

Bell lifted her head and frowned. "Put you to work?"

"No. They wanted to sell me to a guy who liked young boys."

"What?" Bell exploded off the couch. "Sell their child to a pedophile? You can't be serious?"

I sat up. "Bell—"

But she was too steamed to listen. "What was wrong with them?" She threw her arms into the air. "I don't care if they had addictions, they still know right from wrong. They were supposed to protect you." She spun, her face draining of color. "Did... Did he hurt you?"

I grabbed her and pulled her back to me. "No, angel." I settled us back against the couch and into our original position. Her body was tense. "I ran. The cops tried to take me back, but I told them what happened. That was when I ended up in foster care."

"Where are they now?"

"No idea. I haven't ever been interested in finding them."

She sucked in some deep breaths. "And if they're still junkies, and knew you had money..."

"Yeah."

She turned, hugging me hard. "A mother is supposed to sacrifice for her kids. A father's supposed to protect them."

"Not everyone's cut out for it." I smoothed her hair back. "You miss your mom?"

"Yes. We're close. I've sent her a few letters when I could. Dad died from a heart attack when I was in high school. It's just been the two of us for a while."

"You'll see her again, Bell. I promise."

She made a sleepy sound and nuzzled my chest. "She'd like you. She'd say you were tough, caring, and hot."

I felt her body go lax as she fell asleep.

I'd never get to meet Bell's mom. I knew that wasn't in the cards for us.

But I made a vow that one day, Bell would get back to her mother, and they'd both finally be safe.

28

BELL

I was busy checking inventory in the gym. I'd slept surprisingly well after the previous night's drama.

Beau was busy in the back equipment room, doing a weightlifting session with a client. Karina had stopped by for a quick workout and a chat. She'd given me her cellphone number and made me promise we'd get together for lunch soon. I smiled. I think I'd made a friend.

The front door opened, and I paused. I saw Gio tense, as well. He was on guard duty.

"Bell, hi." Mila bustled in, holding some shopping bags and a garment bag. "How are you?" She reached out and gave me a one-armed hug. "Dante told me about the fire."

"I'm fine. Beau and his brothers got to me in time."

Mila squeezed my hand. "You must have been so scared. It's for the best that you're staying with Beau now."

I nodded. "You're up early. Beau told me that you

and Dante are night owls since you both work in a nightclub."

"I had a very good reason to get up early." She held the shopping bags and garment bag out to me. "Shopping. These are for you."

I took them and blinked. "Huh?"

"We're a similar size. Your arms are way more toned than mine so you'll look fabulous in this dress tonight."

She unzipped the garment bag so I could see the black dress inside. It had a square neckline, wide straps over the shoulders and a flirty knee-length skirt. I looked up at her, bemused. "Why do I need a dress?" I couldn't remember the last time I'd worn one.

"For the charity event tonight. At Kav's new distillery."

For a second, I wondered what it would be like to have the money to buy an entire distillery. "Oh. I heard you mention it the other day."

Mila nodded. "For the opening, Kav's holding an event that's raising money for a health program for under-privileged kids."

"I'm not invited."

"You are now. You're Beau's date." She tapped the dress. "I can't wait to watch him watching you in this dress. There are shoes in the bag. Oh, and do smoky eyes but keep your makeup natural."

Still bemused, I shook my head. "Mila, my things went up in smoke. I don't have any makeup."

Hell, I was wearing my hand-washed underwear, and a new set of Hard Burn shirt and shorts, along with running shoes I'd found in the lost property box.

"Lucky for you, your man thought of that." Mila shot me a conspiratorial grin. "He sent me out shopping this morning. Clothes, pajamas, toiletries, makeup. It's all being delivered to his apartment today." She leaned in and smiled. "He especially asked for a few sets of sexy lingerie."

I felt heat in my cheeks.

"And he requested a specific perfume. He didn't know the name, but he said it had to smell like mangoes. I got Marc Jacobs' Daisy Ever So Fresh, so I hope that's all right?"

Tears pricked my eyes, and I nodded. "That's perfect."

"Hey, no crying." She gave me another hug. "You aren't alone anymore. I get how overwhelming that is. When you've been on your own, fighting to survive, it's hard to trust other people. Trust Beau."

I nodded. "Thanks, Mila."

"You are so welcome. See you at lunch."

I blinked. "Lunch?"

"Yes, family lunch. We try to all get together for a meal at least once a week. Beau will bring you over to the main house." She smiled and squeezed my hand.

"Ah, should I bring anything?"

"Just an empty stomach. The brothers' housekeeper Lola is a superb cook. She's making a pot roast, with roast vegetables and Brabant potatoes."

"Okay. Sounds great."

"Oh, and Bell? The event tonight includes a charity fight between Beau and another fighter. Get ready to see him in the ring."

I felt a funny sensation in my belly. "Oh."

Mila waved and walked out.

It looked like smack-dab in the middle of Carr hunting me, I was going to a family lunch followed by a fancy party.

And I was going to get to see Beau fight.

29

BEAU

When I came out of my bathroom with a towel around my waist, and using another to towel off my hair, I found Bell staring at my bed. It was covered in bags.

"Did Mila get everything you need?"

She turned to look at me. "What didn't she buy? Beau, this is too much."

Closing the distance between us, I slung the towel around my neck. I sure as hell liked the way her gaze went straight to my bare chest.

I cupped her jaw, and those fathomless blue eyes met mine. "I don't think it's anywhere near enough."

"Beau—"

"You've been living with nothing for a year. Living out of a damn backpack. You deserve everything that's on that bed."

Her chest hitched. "You're going to make me cry."

"I don't ever want to make you cry." I lowered my

head and brushed my lips over hers. "If I do, you have permission to kick my ass."

That got me a little hiccupping laugh.

"I have something else for you."

"Beau..."

I pulled the silver chain out of my pocket. I'd made a call to a local jeweler today, one that Dante assured me did good work. The idea had popped into my head, and I hadn't been able to shake it. I'd paid extra for him to get the work done today, and Mila had picked it up for me.

Opening my palm, I watched Bell suck in a breath.

The chain had a small pendant dangling off it. It was a tiny little pair of boxing gloves.

"I thought this was perfect for you."

She swallowed. "I love it."

"Turn around."

She gave me her neck, and I slipped the chain on and fastened it. When she turned, she was fingering the pendant.

"Thank you."

I saw the sheen of tears in her eyes.

"No crying or I'll take it back." I kissed her, taking it deeper, pulling in the taste of her. "Wish I had the time to strip you naked and fuck you on top of those bags."

She giggled. And fuck, I loved that sound.

"But if we don't get moving, we'll be late to family lunch, and every single person there will know exactly what made us late."

"Beau, thank you. For saving me last night, and for the new clothes, and...for caring."

My chest squeezed and I heard a warning bell. I was

standing on slippery ground, and if I wasn't careful, I'd be going under for this woman. It was something I couldn't let happen, for her sake.

"You're welcome. Now, change out of your uniform and into something Mila got you. She's got good taste. Then we'll head to lunch."

After I pulled on a dark-blue Henley and jeans, I discovered Mila was a sadist. Bell was wearing blue jeans that definitely weren't from a thrift store. They clung to her body like a happy lover, and the soft, cream sweater slipped off one shoulder, baring smooth skin.

Skin I wanted to kiss.

Her black hair was in a loose braid that rested over her shoulder, and her new necklace lay against her chest. I dragged in a breath and took her hand. "You look gorgeous."

She smoothed her other hand down her thigh. "These jeans feel a bit tight."

"But they look just right."

We headed out of my apartment and out the back way of the building, instead of walking through the gym. I pulled her out onto the sidewalk, scanning around for any sign of Carr. A moment later, we turned left.

"That's Reath and Frankie's warehouse there." I pointed. "Dante and Mila's is that one. Colt and Macy's is next door, and adjoining it is the warehouse that is kind of a central place for all of us. Lola, our housekeeper, lives there. She's also Daisy's nanny."

"What about Kavner and London?"

I pointed to the office tower looming over us. "There.

That's Ignis Tower. Kav's offices are there, and he and London live in the penthouse."

"You guys own a lot of real estate."

"It's our little piece of New Orleans." I pressed a code into the lock on the warehouse door and led Bell inside.

As we walked upstairs, I heard the hubbub of voices. Family lunches were never a quiet affair. We stepped into the large, open-plan kitchen and living area. The central home was done in lots of white and pops of bright colors. It was airy and open, with lots of pot plants that Lola loved to fuss over.

Everyone was crowded around the huge island, while the gray-haired Lola pulled a tray out of the oven.

"Bell!" Daisy skipped over. Her shiny brown hair was in a wonky ponytail. "Come see my cartwheels."

"You can do cartwheels?" Bell grinned at my niece. "Awesome."

"Hey, doesn't your favorite uncle get a kiss first?"

Daisy grinned and threw herself at me. I hugged her close and she smacked a kiss on my cheek.

"Scratchy," she complained.

"You like it."

She fluttered her eyelashes at me. "Uncle Beau, my swear jar is getting very empty."

Damn, I loved this kid. "Really? Well, shit, that's a bloody shame."

Daisy held out a palm, and I fished out some coins for her. "Thanks, Uncle Beau." Then she wriggled to get down, slipping the coins into her pocket. She took Bell's hand. "Come and I'll show you. Daddy pushed the coffee table out of the way so I don't crash into it."

I watched the little girl pull Bell into the living area, then I headed for the kitchen.

"Beauden." Lola smiled at me.

"There's my best girl." I dropped a kiss to her cheek.

She arched an eyebrow. "I have a suspicion I've been replaced as your best girl."

"Never. You'll always be my best girl." I gave an exaggerated sniff. "Especially when you feed me."

She patted my bearded cheek and went back to preparing the food.

I joined my brothers and their women at the island.

"How's Bell doing?" Dante asked.

I glanced at her to see her doing a cartwheel for an ecstatic Daisy. "Okay. A little shellshocked, but she's holding up."

"She's tough," Mila said. "She's had to be to survive this long."

London nodded. "I looked up Carr." She shuddered. "He's a nightmare."

"And now Bell's moved in with you," Colt said.

"She's staying at my place for now. It's the safest option." They all looked at me, and I gritted my teeth. "It's temporary."

"Mmm," Dante murmured.

"It is."

"Did you give her that pretty necklace?" Kav asked.

Shit. I shouldn't have gotten her the necklace. I lowered my voice. "She's twenty-three for God's sake.

Thanks to Carr, she hasn't had a chance to live her life. The last thing she needs is some older guy—"

"You're in your late thirties, Beau," Macy said with a huff. "Hardly ancient."

"And Bell looks happy when she's with you," Mila said. "Why don't you let her decide what she wants."

I grunted. "Here she comes. Let's eat."

"Something smells great," Bell said.

"That's me," Kavner replied. "My new cologne."

London slapped his arm.

"Bell, come meet the best cook in all of Louisiana." I took her hand and waved at Lola. "Lola, this is Bell."

"Lovely to meet you." Lola engulfed her in a big hug. "You're too skinny. You need to eat. Sit, and I'll serve you up a plate."

"Don't eat too much," Mila said. "We have a party tonight, remember?"

Lola made a scoffing sound. "There are plenty of hours between now and your party."

"Lola, I'm staaaarving," Daisy declared.

"Good girl." With a brisk movement, Lola straightened and tightened Daisy's hair. "Wash your hands and up to the table."

As we sat at the large wooden table, passing plates and condiments around, Kavner opened a bottle of wine. There was joking and laughing, and I saw Bell smiling, taking it all in. Daisy only stopped talking to chew and swallow her food.

"Uncle Kav, can I come to your party tonight?" Daisy begged.

"Yes," Kav replied.

"No," Colt countered. "It's for adults, and it's past your bedtime."

The little girl pouted.

"Don't worry." Lola ran a hand over Daisy's ponytail. "It is you and me tonight. I made you something special."

"Gelato!" Daisy cried.

"Yes." Lola smiled at her.

I saw Bell watching the pair, a smile flirting on her lips. I took her hand under the table and rested it on my thigh. She glanced my way, and her smile widened.

Shit. I realized that she fit there. She chatted easily with everyone, and she reminded me of a flower, blooming from the happy atmosphere. She hadn't had any family meals for over a year. Hell, it was just her and her mom, so this was all new to her, yet she fit into the Fury gang like she'd always been there.

I usually didn't drink wine, but I took a gulp now.

Temporary. I had to remember that.

What I needed to focus on was keeping her safe. That was the most important thing.

I exited Beau's Mustang to the wild flash of cameras.

Beau held out his hand and I grabbed it. He led me up the walkway to the huge, brick building down by the river.

Kav's distillery was enormous.

"He bought this entire place?" I said.

"Yes, he's always buying things. He actually has another investor. A businessman from New York." Beau leaned in. "They're planning to make a whole slew of New Orleans-inspired whiskeys. They already have the new name up."

Firebrand Whiskey was up on the side of the building in glowing red neon.

Beau was ignoring all the press taking photos. He was wearing a black suit with a black shirt, and no tie. He looked far more casual than the other guests I saw milling ahead of us, but the look suited him. I knew he'd brought his boxing gear over earlier, after we'd finished with lunch with his family. He and Gio had also brought a portable ring to set up for the fight tonight. I'd stayed at Hard Burn—with Reath for company, a.k.a. my bodyguard.

I was wearing the dress Mila had given me, and it felt a little weird. Not that the dress was weird, it was beautiful, and Mila was right, it suited me. It was just weird to be wearing one. My legs were bare, and I was wearing cute heels. I reached up and touched the pendant around my neck. It probably wouldn't be as fancy as some of the jewelry here tonight, but I loved it.

I glanced at Beau. No man had ever given me jewelry before.

We stepped inside the building.

"Wow." I didn't know where to look first. There was lots of distressed brick, black metal beams, and a concrete floor made the sound echo in the space. Huge glass windows looked into an even larger area. In there were several large metal vats and pipes—things I guessed were part of the distilling process.

"This place is incredible."

"It was going bankrupt, and they were going to have to lay off all their employees. Kav decided to buy it and save everyone's jobs. No doubt he'll turn it around and have it making a profit before we know it. The man has a knack for making money."

I saw lots of people in suits and stylish dresses. I admired one woman's red dress as she walked past on sky-high heels.

"There you guys are." Mila bustled over. She looked stunning in a column of gold silk. Dante followed behind, in a black suit with a snowy-white shirt that looked good with his dark hair and tanned skin.

"I *knew* you'd look fantastic in that dress." She hugged me.

"Thanks, Mila. I haven't worn a dress in a long time."

"It's *you* who looks good," Beau said. "Not the dress." He dropped a kiss on my bare shoulder.

I shivered.

When I looked up, Mila was beaming at us. Dante had a small smile on his rugged face.

"We need drinks," Mila announced. "We have these cool little tasting flights of whiskey, and also some whiskey-inspired cocktails."

"Not for me," Beau said. "Not until after the fight."

I wrinkled my nose. "I'm not really a whiskey drinker."

Mila laughed. "Don't worry, I have some other awesome cocktails on the menu, as well. I'll get you one I know you'll love."

I spotted Macy and Colt, with drinks in hand, across the room. Colt was in a grey suit, and Macy in a pretty green number that suited her. Reath and Frankie were with them. I instantly envied Frankie's electric-blue, maxi-style dress with a halter top.

"Good evening." Drawled Kav as he and London appeared. The pair looked elegant as always. London's dress was an interesting bronze color that clung to her lean body.

"You look gorgeous, Bell," London said.

"Not as gorgeous as you."

London winked at me.

"Everyone, I'd like you to meet my joint partner in Firebrand Whiskey," Kav said.

I turned and saw a handsome man in a tailored suit, who had dark hair and a strong jaw. He reminded me a little of the actor who played Superman. There was an attractive woman at his side, wearing a gorgeous, off-the-shoulder, red dress that hugged her toned body. Her tousled black hair almost brushed her shoulders.

"This is Zane Roth, and his wife, Monroe," Kav announced. "All the way from New York."

"Nice to meet you." Beau shook hands with the man. "You're a long way from home."

The man smiled. "We have to get out of New York sometimes. Don't we, darling?"

Zane Roth. I realized that this man was one of the billionaire bachelors of New York. Three friends who'd made their businesses wildly successful.

I blinked. "I've never met a billionaire before." Oops, the words sort of blurted out of me.

"Yes, you have." London jerked a thumb at Kavner. He winked at me.

God, Kavner was a billionaire? "I've definitely never met two billionaires before."

The woman in the red dress grinned. "I know that feeling well. Zane's besties are billionaires too. I'm Monroe, and it's nice to meet you."

Introductions were made. Everyone was so...nice. So normal. I guess I'd always thought that rich people would be weird. When Mila handed me a cocktail, I took several large sips.

"Well, don't look now, but Bell, you're about to meet your third billionaire," Kavner said. "Dante, Beauden, you remember Ambrose Langston?"

My gaze switched to the man approaching. *Wowser.* He was handsome, in a young-Greek-god kind of way. He looked like he'd been born wearing his expensive suit, that showed off his lean body. He had thick, brown hair, dark eyes that shone with sharp intelligence, and just enough scruff to save him from being pretty.

"It's nice to see you again," he said in a deep voice. He shook hands with the men. "And please, I go by Ro, and usually imagine punching anyone who calls me Ambrose."

"Ro, this is Mila and Bell," Kav introduced us.

Ro Langston inclined his head, then turned to the Roths. "Roth, Monroe."

"Langston," Zane said, while Monroe leaned in to kiss Ro's cheek.

"Ro is a hotel kingpin," London said. "He and Kav are doing some joint projects together."

A small smile tipped up the corner of Ro's lips. "I own Langston Hotels."

My eyes widened. I'd heard of the luxury chain of hotels and resorts. They had properties all around the world.

"Ro and Kav are planning a big new hotel here in New Orleans. That's why he's in town." The corner of London's lips quirked. "And why Kav invited him to come and spend lots of money tonight."

"It's for an excellent charity," Mila said.

Ro nodded. "Then I'll spend big."

"And I want the rest of his money for our new business venture," Kav said. "That's why I'm working with him."

"And I want yours," Ro countered.

The men clinked their glasses together and smiled.

"I need to get ready for the fight." Beau ran a hand down my back. "Mila promised me that she's saved you a good seat."

I shivered, excited to watch him.

"Dante and Mila will take care of you." He dropped a quick kiss to my lips. "See you soon."

"Good luck."

———

IT WAS time for the fight. I followed the Fury brothers and their ladies as we headed for the main part of the distillery.

"May I?" Ambrose Langston offered me his arm.

I assessed him, and decided he was just being polite. Besides, it seemed I liked my men a little more rugged.

I slid my arm through his. "Where are you from, Mr. Langston?"

"Ro, please. Colorado is going to be home for now. I move wherever my work takes me. I just purchased a mountain resort in the Rocky Mountains that I'm planning to overhaul. So, I'm making my base in Denver for now."

"I guess you're planning to transform this resort into the jewel in the Langston crown."

He flashed me a smile that I was certain made many a woman fall at his feet. "Something like that."

We entered the heart of the distillery. I glanced up at

the big tanks, but then my gaze was riveted on the spot-lights highlighting the boxing ring.

I felt a spurt of excitement. I couldn't wait to watch Beau in action.

"It's time for the most exciting part of the evening to start," an announcer said over the loudspeakers. I recognized his voice from one of the local radio stations. The lights flashed. "Please take your seats, ladies and gentlemen. The main attraction will be starting now. Don't forget our silent auction. There are amazing items up for grabs, and all the proceeds go to an incredibly good cause, supporting the healthcare of underprivileged children."

Mila waved a hand. "Our seats are over here."

We took our front-row seats in the lines of chairs set up around the boxing ring. Mila sat on one side of me, and Ro on the other.

Then I watched as Beau came out of a doorway, walking toward the ring. He wore dark-blue shorts and a boxing robe. The crowd went wild, cheering his name. He lifted a gloved hand into the air.

"And here is our local fighter, one of New Orleans' favorite sons, Beauden Fury," the announcer said.

My gaze was locked on him. He climbed into the ring, and butterflies filled my belly.

"And our competitor this evening, all the way from Miami, Deon Jones."

A heavily muscled black man in red boxing gear strolled in. I swallowed. He looked strong and fit, and I guessed he was ten years younger than Beau.

In the ring, the men both shed their boxing robes. Gio stood at Beau's corner and took the robe. The two men talked for a moment, and Beau nodded. I drank in his muscular body and felt tingles low down in my belly. I pressed my legs together.

Then the bell rang. "Let the fight begin!"

I sucked in a breath. Beau charged forward—with no dancing or cautious moves. He threw the first punch.

Wow. This looked nothing like our training.

Muscles bulged, and bodies flexed. I tried to take note of all the punches and combos they were doing, but I got lost in simply watching the vital beauty of Beau fighting.

It was all power. All rough grace.

He took a few hits, but barely reacted. His opponent might be good and younger, but he was clearly outclassed.

The crowd cheered and booed with each hit.

I watched Beau land a punch to his opponent's head. A part of me wanted to wince in sympathy for Deon.

But all my focus was on Beau.

He was so beautiful. So strong. His skin shone with perspiration, outlining all his muscles and highlighting his tattoos. I felt a pulse between my legs, and I fought not to squirm in my seat.

The minutes ticked by. I'd known that Beau was an amazing fighter, but seeing him in action was something else. I'd never get enough of watching him. He hammered a blow into his opponent, then followed through with another punch to the head. I watched Deon's big body jerk. His head flew to the side, then he tumbled and hit the mat. He tried to get up, but slumped back down.

The crowd cheered and clapped.

I sat there, my heart beating hard in my chest.

Beau bounced a little on his feet, watching as the referee counted to ten. Then the ref grabbed Beau's arm and raised it into the air.

"The winner! Beauden Fury."

"He's still got it," Dante said over the roar of the crowd.

Beau waved, then his gaze searched the seats, and locked on me.

Oh. There was heat in his gaze. It was scalding, and my panties were damp in an instant.

He climbed out of the ring and gave the fans another wave. The announcer was saying something, but I couldn't hear it over the roar in my ears.

Mila leaned in. "The changing rooms were set up back there, through that door." She pointed to the doorway where Beau had disappeared.

I nodded.

"Go," she said.

I rose. "I should...um...help Beau."

Dante's lips quirked. "Yeah, I reckon he'd appreciate that."

I nodded and worked my way along the rows of chairs. By the time I reached the doorway, I was half jogging.

I moved down the corridor and spotted two open doors. When I peered in the first, it was empty, but a bag and gear lay inside. I also saw Deon Jones' name taped on the door.

Quickly, I moved to the next room. The name Fury was taped on this one.

Heart beating hard, I stepped into the doorway. Beau was sitting on a chair, his gear on the table. He was taking tape off one hand.

Then his head jerked up, and his gaze caught mine.

Nerves and desire collided inside me. The way Beau stared at me—this big, beautiful man—made me feel stripped bare.

I stepped inside and closed the door behind me.

His broad chest heaved, then he rose.

I crossed the room fast, my heels clicking on the floor.

"*Bell*," he growled.

I leaped at him. He caught me. Of course he did, he always would.

He made a deep, masculine sound and then his mouth was on mine. The kiss was hard and rough.

Exactly what I needed.

My hands speared into his hair, and I kissed him back. I poured all my pent-up desire into it. He smelled like healthy sweat and Beau, but I didn't care that he'd just finished a fight. I wanted him too much.

He carried me several steps, and pressed my back to the wall. His hands bunched up the skirt of my dress.

"Need to fuck you." His voice was so low I could barely understand him.

I reached under my skirt, and nudged my panties down.

Beau did the rest, and I felt the lace slip down my legs. I kicked my heels off.

He shoved my skirt out of his way, and I felt him push his boxing shorts down.

"You ready for me?" His voice was like gravel.

Even now, in the throes of one of the hottest moments of my life, he was looking after me.

"Yes. The fight...I'm wet."

That got me a primal growl. He hitched me higher and shoved between my legs.

With one hard thrust, he filled me.

I cried out, clawing at his bare shoulders. I felt him. The sweet sting of taking him.

Then he started to slam into me.

I held on, reveling in each hard thrust. Each hard claim. His big hands slid under my ass, and I felt the tape still on one of them. It scraped across my sensitive skin. I wrapped my legs around him as tight as I could.

My moans filled the room, along with Beau's grunts. Every hard stroke felt like a possession. I whimpered.

"Get there, Bell," he ordered.

It was all I needed. I came, my orgasm as strong and rough as Beau's thrusts.

I screamed.

Then he pumped into me again, pinning me hard to the wall. His groan was loud as he came. Every muscle in his body strained.

Then finally, there was just our heavy breathing, and the rapid drum of my heart. Pleasure tingled through every part of me. I wasn't sure if I'd be able to walk again, but it was worth it.

"I really liked watching you fight," I said huskily.

His laugh was low and rough. He pulled me away from the wall, holding my weight easily.

He kissed me. It was the opposite of the fast,

desperate sex we'd just had. The kiss was slow and lazy, but still a claiming.

"I messed you up," he said.

"Makeup and hair can be fixed." I had some essentials in my handbag.

He set me down, and ran a thumb over my lips. "I didn't use a condom."

Oh. Now I was aware of the stickiness between my thighs.

"You on birth control?"

I shook my head. It was hard to get medication when you were on the run.

"I'm clean," he told me.

I nodded. "Me too."

His rough fingers ran along my cheekbones. "Whatever happens, we'll deal. Together."

He didn't seem upset, so I nodded.

He pressed another kiss to my lips. "My angel. So damn sweet. There's a bathroom through there." He nodded toward an adjoining door. "Clean up and redo your makeup. Then I'll shower and change. After that, we can get back to the party and I'll buy you a drink."

31

BEAU

W hen we rejoined the party, it was pretty obvious I'd fucked Bell. Her dress was rumpled, her hair was no longer smooth and sleek, and her cheeks were pink.

But she was smiling. I watched her as she nodded at Mila, and accepted a cocktail. My brothers' women were all around her, chatting and laughing.

Accepting her.

They'd miss her when she was gone.

So would I.

My hand fisted beside my thigh. I couldn't keep her. It wasn't an option.

Memories of my parents, and that rat-infested house that reeked of sweat, drugs, and trash hit me hard. What they were ended with me. I wouldn't pass it on.

Yet you just fucked Bell without a condom.

My gut twisted. I'd never gone without a rubber. Having kids wasn't ever going to happen.

It was just once, so hopefully we'd be okay. I wouldn't

drag Bell down with my baggage. I wanted her safe and free to do what she wanted. To fly high. Without the weight of Chandler Carr on her shoulders. Then she wouldn't need to learn to fight anymore.

She wouldn't need a scarred, tattooed, former foster kid who came from trash.

I knew what I was. Who I was. And I was comfortable with my life.

Then why do you like knowing it's your come inside her right now?

Fuck.

Ignoring the voice in my head, I took a large swig of my whiskey.

"Great fight, Beau." Kav appeared. "I won good money on you from Zane."

I glanced at Roth and his wife.

The businessman held up a hand. "I knew you'd win, but I was happy to lose knowing that the money goes to charity. Well done, it was a great fight."

"It was an excellent fight," Ambrose Langston said. "You have a hell of a right hook."

"You box?" I knew better than to assume that because he was rich and handsome he was the stereotypical billionaire that just sat behind a desk. Kav had taught me that.

"Only a little. I move around a lot with work, to wherever my latest acquisition is. But I can always take a punching bag with me."

"You ever want to work out here in New Orleans, drop by Hard Burn."

He inclined his head. "Thanks."

I looked over at Bell again. She and Macy were laughing at something. I was glad she was having fun.

The others moved on, leaving me, Colt, Reath, and Dante cradling our whiskey glasses.

"So, Bell looks...rumpled," Dante murmured.

I grunted.

"You're head over heels for her," he said. "When are you going to admit it?"

My fingers tightened on my glass. "I told you, it's short-term."

"Does she know that?"

Anger felt like a hard knock to my gut. It made me feel like punching something. "Yes. When I get her free of Carr, she'll go back to Texas."

"She's falling in love with you, Beau," Reath said. "As a man who's just been through it, I know the look."

Now, I felt... Hell, I didn't know what I felt. "I... can't."

"Can't what?" Dante said. "Keep her? Claim her? Love her?"

"Goddammit." My arm snapped out and I gripped the front of Dante's shirt.

My brother didn't react, his gaze trained on my face. "You're already in love with her."

"I'm *not* inflicting my history on her."

Dante made an angry sound. "Not this again. Fuck your parents. You're a good man. Hell, Beau, if we go with your logic, none of us deserve the women we've claimed."

I shook my head.

"You can't have it both ways," Colt said. "Either we're

trash with bad bloodlines, or we're the men we made ourselves into."

For a second, I let myself imagine my life with Bell in it.

Imagined my seed between her legs taking root, and imagined her round with our child.

Shit. Fuck.

Then across the room, I saw Bell stiffen. She was looking through the crowd, frowning. What was she looking at?

Then she set her glass down, and started shoving her way through the throng of people.

"Something's wrong." I shoved my glass at Dante, and charged after her.

I lost sight of her, and my chest squeezed. *Where the hell was she?*

Had she seen Carr? I knew security was tight. PSS was running it, and Reath only hired the best. Carr couldn't be here.

"Beau?" Ro Langston materialized next to me, his brow creased. "Is everything all right?"

"I'm looking for Bell."

"I saw her before. Maybe she went through that doorway?"

Without a word, I wrenched the door open. I was barely aware of Ro following me down the long corridor. There were some offices and storage rooms, but no sign of Bell.

"What's wrong?" The hotelier's tone was no-nonsense. A man used to dealing with problems.

"Bell has a serial killer hunting her. Chandler Carr."

"Jesus." The billionaire sounded shocked.

"She wouldn't follow him or disappear for no reason."

My cellphone rang. Dante's name flashed up on the screen. I pressed it to my ear.

"Beau? What's going on?"

"I'm in a service corridor with Ro. Bell came this way. I think she must have seen Carr. Tell Reath to alert his guys."

"On it. Beauden, be careful."

I turned the corner and still saw no sign of her. "Bell!" My bellow echoed off the walls.

We passed through a doorway and came out onto a loading dock. There were huge roller doors where the trucks would come in to load up the whiskey. They were all closed.

"Bell!" I called again.

The place was silent. The kind of silence that raised the hairs on the back of the neck. My gaze skimmed several racks of empty whiskey bottles, clearly ready to be filled at some stage.

Beside me, Ro was alert, scanning the shadows.

Suddenly, a shadow flew out of the darkness. He swung an empty whiskey bottle at Ro.

The billionaire dodged.

The attacker whirled, and I noted that the man was wearing a server's uniform.

And a creepy clown mask.

"Carr," I growled. "Where is she?"

He darted out of reach, and I followed, swinging my fist. I landed a blow to the man's head, watching with pleasure as it snapped back.

ANNA HACKETT

This was the man who'd traumatized Bell. Who'd murdered her friend, and hunted Bell like an animal.

"Beau, watch out!" Ro cried.

A glass bottle was swinging directly for my head. I threw myself sideways, and Carr and the bottle brushed past me. But the bastard whirled, smashed the bottle against a rack, and the end of it shattered. Then he threw it at me.

This time, I was too slow to move. It slammed into my chest.

I staggered back, pain reverberating through my torso. The bottle hit the ground and splintered. The asshole darted away, disappearing into the darkness. I felt blood bloom on my shirt.

"Bell." Panic gripped me. *What had Carr done with her?*

"Beau, I'm here." She ran out of the doorway we'd come out of, out of breath. "I thought I saw Carr, but I didn't follow him. Dante said you'd come this way."

She was safe. He didn't have her.

I strode to her and pulled her into my arms. "You didn't follow him?"

"Of course I didn't follow him. I was looking for you. He was wearing the same uniform as the servers."

I hugged her harder.

"Beau, your chest's bleeding."

"Carr threw a broken bottle at me."

She froze. "It was him? He's here?"

I nodded.

"He went out this way," Ro called out.

I saw the billionaire standing at an external door beside the roller doors.

"Beau?" Reath, one of his men, and my brothers rushed through the doorway.

"Carr's here," I said.

With Bell tucked close to my side, I walked over to Ro.

Reath and his security guard went first. They opened the door and glanced outside. A security light cast a weak light around the external loading dock.

"What the fuck?" Ro muttered.

Reath muttered a curse.

Bell pushed forward and sucked in a sharp breath.

A dead cat lay sprawled on the ground. With its eyes gouged out.

Fuck.

And beside it, was a red boxing glove that had been torn to shreds.

Bell's face drained of color. "No," she whispered.

"Girly, you need to slow down, or you'll burn out."

I looked up at Gio. My fingers tightened on the cleaning cloth in my hand. I'd been cleaning every nook and cranny of Hard Burn. I felt Beau's gaze on me, and looked past Gio. He was in one of the rings training a client, but I'd felt him watching me all morning.

I blew out a breath. "I'm good, Gio, I promise."

The older man looked worried, but nodded. "I'm going to order us all subs for lunch." He pointed a finger at me. "And you'll eat it all." He stomped off.

I sat down on one of the benches and sighed. I was tired. After the party at the distillery, and the run-in with Carr, I hadn't been able to sleep.

Beau had held me tight, but all I'd seen in my mind was that shredded glove.

It was a threat.

Against Beau.

If he got hurt...

I swallowed. I couldn't let that happen. Beauden Fury meant too much to me.

I froze. I was falling in love with him. My heart sped up. Of course I was. I'd never met a guy like him before. One so real, so protective. He'd overcome so much to become the man he was. I'd never wanted a man the way I wanted Beau.

I looked up and he was watching me again. I managed a smile.

Last night, I'd thought about leaving. But the idea of leaving Beau hurt so much. I mean, I wasn't sure where this thing between us was headed, but it felt good. Right.

And Beau was right—it was time to stop running. Here, with Beau and his brothers, I had the best chance ever of stopping Carr.

I stood up. Time to get back to work. As I grabbed my cloth and spray, I wondered where Karina was today. She usually liked to get her workout in by now.

I went through the gym equipment, cleaning stuff I knew I'd already cleaned, but the work kept my mind off everything. I heard a cellphone ring and watched Beau say something to his client, then pull out his phone. He usually didn't answer calls when he was training, but after last night, he was keeping his phone close. He pressed it to his ear.

A moment later, his big body froze. That stillness made me queasy. I kept watching as he cursed and raked a hand through his hair.

Something was wrong.

I walked closer, my stomach filling with knots.

"Yeah. Fuck. Who found her?" He paused. "God-dammit. Yeah, I will. Thanks, Simon."

Beau's detective friend. My throat went dry. I took another step and Beau swiveled, his gray gaze on me.

I watched the storm clouds fill his eyes.

"What happened?" I asked.

He sighed, nodded to his client, then slipped out of the ring. "Let's go to my office—"

"No, Beau. Just tell me. It's something to do with Carr."

Another sigh. "Yeah."

I swallowed the lump in my throat. "Tell me."

Beau's face twisted, and I knew

"He killed again," I whispered.

"Angel." He gripped my arms. "I'm sorry."

Some poor woman was dead. Some poor woman had died, alone and terrified.

Because Carr couldn't get to me.

"Bell." He tipped my face up with his fingertips. "It was Karina."

Shock slammed into me like lightning. I shook my head. "No."

I couldn't compute.

"Her mom found her at her apartment."

I stepped back, the cloth and spray bottle falling from my hands. "No."

A woman I knew. A young woman I'd befriended. A nice woman who was so full of life. I tasted bile in my mouth and felt sick.

Carr had targeted Karina because of me. He must've seen us talking.

Oh, God.

I whirled and raced for Beau's apartment.

"Bell!"

I ignored Beau, ran up the stairs, and into his place. I didn't pause. I ran up to his bedroom, and straight into the bathroom.

I dropped to my knees in front of the toilet, and vomited up my breakfast.

Karina. Sweet, funny Karina who brought me cookies and smoothies. Raped, tortured, killed. *My fault. All my fault.*

I knelt there, and heaved again.

"Bell."

Beau's arms moved around me, his big body pressing against my back. I squeezed my eyes shut. I couldn't feel any worse.

"She's dead?" I whispered.

"Yes, angel. I'm sorry."

Emotion welled inside me. I pushed to my feet, and then at the sink, rinsed my mouth out. Then I swept past Beau.

I had to go.

I found the nice bag Mila had gotten for me when she'd done the shopping, and started pulling out some of the clothes she'd bought for me. I shoved them into the bag.

Big hands caught mine.

"No," he said.

"I have to leave."

"*No,*" he said again. He swung me around to face him. "You are *not* leaving me."

"It's to *protect* you. And your brothers. And Mila and Macy and—" my voice broke. "Beau, I couldn't bear if he hurt you, or your family." Tears filled my eyes, spilling down my cheeks. "I can't bear knowing that Karina is dead because of me."

"She's dead because of Carr. *He's* to blame. You're a victim."

That didn't matter. Right now, all I could feel was misery and pain.

"Angel?"

Then I was in Beau's arms. I gripped him tight, like he was an anchor that would keep me in place. I felt like this nightmare would finally sweep me away and drag me under.

"You're *not* leaving." Beau's tone was rigid and unbending. "We're stopping him, and I will protect you. I told you, I'm bigger and meaner than Chandler Carr."

I clung to him.

Then he pulled back, his face filled with determination. "And you're stronger than him, too. You want to stop him?"

I nodded. I wanted nothing more than to stop Carr.

"The only way to do that is if we do it together. I learned that when I met my brothers, that you can do so much more when you aren't alone. When you have people to depend on and who have your back."

My fingers dug into his arms. "You can't get hurt."

"I won't. And nor will you. Bell, I promise to have your back."

I nodded. "Together."

BEAU

I stood in the computer room at Phoenix Security Services, my hands on my hips. One of Reath's guys, Lincoln, was at Hard Burn with Bell. There were two more of Reath's men outside, keeping an eye out for Carr.

It made me itchy to be away from her. God, I wanted to pummel Carr into a pulp. My anger was a hot, sharp ball in my gut.

Poor Karina. An innocent woman killed for some sicko's pleasure. And to hurt Bell.

Carr had known this would devastate her.

"Bell blames herself for Karina's murder," I said.

Reath made an unhappy sound. "There's only one person to blame—the man who killed her."

"Carr wanted to hurt Bell, and he knew this would cut deep." I shoved a hand through my hair for about the hundredth time. "Karina was sweet. She didn't deserve this."

My brothers all looked pissed. Colt leaned against the wall, the image of cool, but radiating energy. Dante sat in a chair, his face dark. Reath was by the computer, his arms crossed. And Kavner was perched against the desk.

"If it's any consolation at all, Karina Merrick's death was quick," Simon said.

The detective had joined us, and wasn't hiding his anger. I knew he hated losing a woman on his watch, and wanted this serial killer stopped. Probably even more than we did.

A muscle ticked in Simon's jaw. "Carr broke his MO of spending hours torturing and raping his victim."

"Maybe something spooked him?" Reath suggested. "Or he's getting sloppy."

Which meant he was taking more risks, and getting more dangerous.

"We have to find him," I said, jaw tight. "Bell is his target. He got too damn close last night."

"He's clearly good at blending in," Reath said. "He looks...normal. Innocuous. He'd also changed his hair and eye color, and used a fake ID last night. That's how he ended up on the catering staff." Reath's jaw worked. "It won't happen again."

"He's not just after Bell." Dante looked up. "The boxing glove was a threat."

"Oh, he's welcome to come at me." My hands flexed.

"You've got to keep your cool, Beau," Reath said. "Don't underestimate him."

I blew out a breath. "I won't."

"He wants to hurt Bell," Dante said. "Hurting you would do that."

"How do we find the bastard?" I clipped out.

"I've given out his description," Simon said. "If any cop in New Orleans spots him, we'll know."

"He's probably changed his hair color again or is changing his appearance when he's out in public," Reath said. "If he changes his facial features enough, we won't get any hits on facial recognition."

"And he wears that damn clown mask," I added.

"We did get a report of a guy matching his description staying at a cheap hotel near the airport," Simon said. "He paid for three nights with cash, but left. There was no sign of him when my guys got there. The room was wiped clean."

Colt nodded. "He's probably hopping around cheap hotels who don't keep good records. Just a few days, then on to the next place. It's a common tactic for the guys I track who skip bail."

"He'll come at Bell again," I said.

In my head, I saw her stricken face when she'd learned about Karina. For her, it was like losing her friend Allie all over again.

Then I pictured her trying to pack to leave.

Leave New Orleans.

Leave me.

My muscles tightened. Carr had to be stopped, once and for all. "I won't let him touch one fucking hair on her head."

"We know." Dante rose and clamped a hand on my arm. "When our women were in trouble, you helped keep them safe, and we'll do the same for Bell. We know how important it is. How important she is."

I wanted to say that it was temporary, and to not read too much into it, but right now, I couldn't.

Right now, all I could focus on was keeping her safe. And holding her close as she grieved again.

"When she heard about Karina, she fell apart." My mouth flattened. "She wanted to run again."

"That's not going to dissuade Carr," Simon said. "He'll keep hunting her."

"And we're going to stop him." I met all their gazes. "He's going to feel the full force of the Fury brothers."

My brothers all nodded.

"And you have my support," Simon said. "I'm not going to let a serial killer run loose in our city." Then he slid his hands into the pockets of his trousers. "I know you don't want to hear this, but it's likely that the best way to find Carr is through Bell."

I stiffened. "Use her as bait? Hell, no."

Simon held up a hand. "That's not what I meant. But we need to prepare her for when he approaches her again. If we can, we can use her to get Carr out in the open. So we can finally stop him, and get Bell safe."

Get Bell safe.

That was what I wanted most of all.

I nodded. "I'll talk with her." I already knew she'd fight. She had some decent skills from our training now. She'd do anything to stop Carr.

"We need to be ready," Reath said. "This motherfucker isn't going to go down easily."

I made a fist. "His downfall will be that he'll try to taunt and torment Bell. He can't help himself. He gets off on it. We need to use that against him."

And I needed to prepare her for anything. I'd do everything I could to make sure she wasn't helpless.

Reath nodded. "Let's take this asshole down."

My brothers all nodded.

Watch out, Carr. The Fury brothers are coming for you.

"Good job on those posters, girly."

I looked up at Gio and tried to smile. "Thanks, G."

I'd spent the morning revamping the reception area to keep busy. I'd added some boxing and fitness photos to the wall.

"They look great." He scratched the back of his neck. "You doing okay? Beau told me about Karina. Poor girl."

Pain—raw and cutting—hit me.

"I'm not okay yet," I whispered.

He nodded. "But you will be. You're strong. And Beau will help you."

Tears pricked my eyes, and I nodded. Gio was another connection. Another reminder that I wasn't alone.

"Thanks, Gio."

He gripped my shoulder. "Karina was a good girl. She wouldn't want you doing something stupid like blaming yourself."

"I know."

With a nod, he headed toward the boxing rings.

I headed back to Beau's office. I spotted my body-guard, Lincoln, sitting on a bench nearby. He had shaggy blond-brown hair and looked like he should be on a surf-board catching a wave. When our gazes met, he gave me a chin lift. I waved back.

In the office, I sat in Beau's creaky chair and opened the laptop. I was setting up a new bill payment system online. That way we could avoid Beau having piles of invoices on his desk. In the short time I'd been at Hard Burn, I'd learned that the man hated doing any sort of paperwork.

I tapped my finger on the desk. I liked this. I liked helping with the business side of the gym. I could see the attraction of running your own business. It was what I'd been studying at college.

If Beau was right, and we stopped Carr, I could go back to college. I could finish my degree.

And what about you and Beau?

I worried my bottom lip. I wasn't sure, but I knew we had something. Something special.

I was falling for the man.

Once we didn't have Carr hanging over our heads, I'd talk to him.

Beau was currently at Reath's security office. I knew they were discussing how to find Carr. I'd wanted to go, but Beau had been firm that I had to stay at the gym. To be honest, right now, I didn't want to think about Carr.

I got busy, and thirty minutes later, Beau returned. His face was so serious that it made my chest lock.

"I'm out of here," Lincoln called out. "Bye, Bell."

"Bye." My gaze stayed on Beau. "Thanks, Lincoln." I rose from the desk chair. "Hey."

He closed the door, and the look on his face made it hard to breathe. A part of me was afraid he was going to send me away. Tell me he was done dealing with all this trouble.

"We're looking for Carr," he said. "The New Orleans PD, Reath's team, Colt."

I swallowed the lump in my throat and nodded.

"He's good at hiding."

"I know. I'm sorry, Beau—"

He closed the distance between us and gripped my arms. "You have *nothing* to be sorry about."

I leaned into him, and let his warmth seep into my cold skin. "It doesn't feel like that."

He smoothed a hand up my back. "I know he'll come at you again."

I looked up and saw his jaw working.

"We already knew that." I smoothed my hand over his beard.

"You are *not* alone," Beau growled. "Promise me, we work together. We bring Carr down together."

I nodded and felt warmth unfurl in my chest.

"Good." He pulled me up on my toes and planted a deep kiss on my lips. "Now, I think I have a client to train."

"You do. And I'll finish with this mess." I waved at his untidy desk.

He glanced at the paperwork and laptop. "It's all yours."

I laughed as he headed out.

The rest of the day was uneventful. A part of me kept thinking Carr would do something, and it left me feeling edgy and unsettled.

"You're safe in here with Beau," I murmured to myself.

The gym was busy now. All the machines and rings were full. I saw that Beau was doing an intense training session with one of his regular clients.

I grabbed a box of gear from the storage cupboard and headed to the ladies change room. I'd ordered a few things to brighten the space. I had some nice hand soap and shampoo, and a few things to make the space more feminine and welcoming.

The change room was empty, except for a few workout bags resting out on the benches. I carried my box in, set it on the counter by the sinks, and got to work nailing some posters up. They showed women of various sizes in workout gear—boxing, lifting weights, stretching.

I set the hammer down and studied my handiwork. *Nice.* I straightened one frame and grinned. They looked perfect.

Next, I refilled the hand wash, and spritzed some air freshener that smelled like flowers. Very nice.

I headed into the showers with the new shower gel and shampoo that didn't smell like something a man would use. I filled up one dispenser when I heard a noise out in the main change room.

"Hello? I won't be a minute. I'm almost finished in here." I finished topping up the rest of the dispensers and walked out. "You can use the showers now."

There was no one there.

I frowned. *Weird.* I went over to stack some fresh towels on the shelves.

Another sound echoed through the space. It sounded like the scrape of a boot on the floor.

I spun. I didn't see anybody.

"Hello?" My heart started pumping. "Who's there?"

Moving quickly, I dashed for my box, and snatched up the hammer. I gripped it tight.

I wasn't going to run.

I was going to stand my ground.

I walked toward the lockers. There was no sign of anyone. I turned slowly. The change room was empty except for me.

But someone had been here. I was sure of it.

That's when I saw a locker door was ajar.

My locker.

Swallowing, I walked slowly toward it. I saw my gear was inside and nothing looked like it was missing.

I lowered the hammer.

That's when I saw the note sticking out from under a shirt.

Sound roared in my ears. The others had all burned up in the fire. Slowly, I picked up the piece of paper.

My lips pressed into a flat line. I pulled in a deep breath and read it.

The boxer is dead if you don't do what I want. It won't be a slow or easy death.

You can save him, if you come alone and don't tell anyone.

There was an address scrawled on the bottom.

It was Carr's writing.

Beau. He'd threatened Beau.

I raced out of the change room and back into the gym. I paused and saw Beau was still in one of the rings. I pressed a hand to my chest, over my racing heart. I watched him as he and the man he was training traded punches. I loved that primal, masculine beauty of his. I loved watching him spar.

I couldn't imagine a world without Beauden Fury in it.

He'd survived so much and deserved a beautiful life.

I looked at the note again.

I knew what I had to do.

I crumpled the paper in my palm.

———

MY HANDS CLENCHED on the steering wheel of Beau's Mustang.

I was really nervous. It had been a long time since I'd driven, plus it was in a dark area that I didn't know.

My heart was pounding, and my hands were sweaty. I felt like I'd been driving for hours.

I was finally going to confront Chandler Carr.

I was heading to an address outside of New Orleans. I'd left the city lights behind a long time ago, and now there were dark trees all around me. It was remote out here, and I couldn't see any houses.

I swallowed. Beau would be so worried.

My hands flexed. I had to stick to the plan.

This ended tonight.

I leaned over and checked my cellphone. I had the map app open, and I could see I was getting close.

Hunching over the wheel, I searched for the turn to my destination. *There.* I barely spotted the overgrown driveway. I turned, the tires crunching on gravel. There were no lights anywhere. I dragged in a few deep breaths, nerves alive in my stomach.

Tonight, I was going to face the nightmare who'd stolen Allie and Karina from me. Who'd hunted me for over a year.

A cabin came into view.

I slowed and stared at the house. It was made of old, weathered wood, with a sagging front porch. There were no lights on, and bushes had grown up around it, giving it a wild, abandoned feel.

Of course, Carr wanted to make this as scary as possible.

I pulled the car to a stop. Thank God I hadn't crashed or scratched Beau's baby. I turned off the engine and sat there in the darkness, staring at the dilapidated cabin.

Fear was a big, hard ball in my throat. But I felt steady. I had to do this.

I checked my watch. Almost time.

I reached up and gripped the chain around my neck, my fingers closing over the boxing gloves pendant. Since I'd met him, Beau had given me so much: trust, desire, confidence.

And the skills to fight.

I love you, Beau.

I checked my watch again, watching the minute hand tick. Time for me to end this.

Pushing open the door, I stepped out. I reached for the flashlight I'd brought with me and flicked it on. Carefully, I followed the beam of light, shoes crunching as I walked toward the cabin. The bushes shivered in the light breeze, cutting through my jeans and T-shirt, like they knew something bad was coming.

I stepped onto the rickety porch, boards creaking under my shoes. I pulled open a torn screen door, and saw the wooden front door was ajar.

My chest hitched. Carr was here, somewhere.

I nudged the door wider and shone the flashlight around. The front room was empty, the floorboards covered in a layer of dust and old leaves. There was torn, old wallpaper on the walls.

Then the beam of light reflected off something and I tensed. I blew out a breath. It was just a grimy, old mirror on the wall.

Suddenly, a masculine laugh echoed through the house.

I stiffened. Carr. Taunting me. My jaw tightened and it took everything I had to step inside.

You can do this, Bell.

"I'm here, Carr." And I'm not afraid of you.

There was no sign of him. As I walked, the floorboards creaked under me. I moved my arm, waving the flashlight around.

"Carr!"

He was a coward. I realized now that he always waited until he could surprise his victim. Isolate her, lull her, then attack.

I sure as hell wouldn't be lulled.

I spotted something on the floor.

Keeping my flashlight beam on it, I walked over. It was a photo. I picked it up and bit my lip.

It showed a smiling Karina leaving Hard Burn.

"I'm so sorry, Karina," I whispered, my heart squeezing.

I continued into another empty room. There was just more dust, and a huge cobweb covering one wall.

There was also another photo on the floor, and I steeled myself.

This one was of Allie.

She was smiling right at the camera. Her red hair was thick and shiny.

Emotion flooded me.

"I miss you so much, Al." I slipped the photos into my pocket. Carr couldn't have them. I wouldn't leave them here.

The beam of the flashlight hit another photo, and my heart kicked in my chest. This one was of me and Beau.

I was in his arms, smiling up at him, and I realized how I felt about him was stamped all over my face. It was from the party at the distillery.

Beau's eyes had been gouged out of the photo.

Heat rushed through me. *You won't get to hurt him, asshole.*

Or me.

"Just come out, Carr. I know you like to grandstand, but quite frankly, I'm sick of it."

Creak.

I spun, but saw nothing.

"You really are a coward, aren't you?"

"The little rabbit isn't running anymore."

I turned and saw a dark silhouette detach from one of the walls.

Lifting the flashlight, I aimed it right at his face.

How could such a slim, unassuming man be so evil?

"Did fucking that big thug make you feel strong?" Carr said.

I stayed silent.

The serial killer stepped closer. "He's not here to help you now."

Because I could damn well help myself. "I look forward to when they give you the death penalty," I said. "I'll come to watch. Allie and Karina will be watching too."

Carr laughed. "They'll never catch me." He lifted his arm. He was holding a knife. The long blade shone in the light.

My gut clenched. *Stay calm. Stick to the plan.*

"I'm going to watch *you* die, little Bell. We're going to have so much fun."

The fear came. It spread, tangling around my throat, but I controlled it. I heard Beau's deep voice in my head. *Assess for weaknesses, use your advantages.*

I pulled in a slow breath. "I don't plan to die tonight."

The man who'd hunted me for so long smiled. "We'll see." He charged at me. Fast.

My adrenaline spiked. He slashed out with the knife, but my training kicked in. I dodged, then landed a perfect punch to his face.

He grunted and stepped back. My knuckles hurt like

hell, but I kept my gaze on him. I stepped forward and rammed an uppercut into his stomach.

He was soft.

Realization rocketed through me. He wasn't strong, and he didn't know how to fight. He just overwhelmed women who were less strong than him.

Carr made an angry sound and swung again. I blocked him and rammed two punches into his face. His nose crunched, and blood poured down his mouth and chin. He let out a screech.

I danced back, keeping my weight balanced.

"What's wrong, Carr? You don't like it when you take on someone stronger than you?"

He roared and ran at me.

I whirled. The knife nicked my side, but I spun again, moving in behind him. I landed punches to his kidneys. Then I kicked him.

He ran headfirst into the wall.

"You're not so scary now," I taunted.

He spun, an enraged look contorting his face. "You won't be so confident when I slide this blade between your ribs." He held the knife up and ran at me.

I darted to the side, and kept moving. I had him. I could take him down.

Then my shoe hit an uneven floorboard, and I tripped.

Shit. I fell flat on my back.

A slow smile curled Carr's lips. He advanced.

Shit. Shit. *Shit.*

He slashed down with the knife, just as I lifted both feet and kicked at him.

"You'll die here tonight," he roared. His arm came down again.

I kicked him again, trying to knock the knife away.

"I'll rape you, I'll slit you open. Your blood will cover the walls and floor."

"Fuck you, Carr. Tonight, you don't win. You're going down."

He laughed. "Do you really think you can stop me?"

"No. Not alone."

He hesitated, a frown forming.

Then the front and back doors burst open.

A fierce-looking Beau charged through the front door, Reath and Kavner right behind him. Dante and Colt came in through the back.

They all had guns trained on Carr.

The serial killer's face went slack with shock.

"It's better when you have a team." I rose and looked at Beau. "When you aren't alone."

35

BEAU

I shot a quick glance at Bell. She was alive, her face filled with that determination of hers.

There was blood on her shirt.

My muscles tightened. Carr would pay for that. Along with everything else.

The killer looked around, his gaze settling on me.

"You told him?" he snarled. "You didn't come alone."

"Yeah, you wanted her alone, didn't you?" I took a step forward. "You wanted easy prey. You're a coward."

"I'm not easy prey," Bell said. "I've learned a few things lately, the biggest one being that having someone at your back makes all the difference."

"Get on your knees, Carr," I growled.

The man hesitated, and I knew he was looking for a way out.

"Now!"

Lightning fast, he lunged at Bell.

"Don't fire!" I cried. "Don't hit Bell."

But my girl wasn't afraid. Her punch snapped Carr's head back. There was no fear on her face.

Damn, she was something.

Quickly, I tucked my gun into the waistband of my cargo pants and advanced. I wanted to use my fists. I wanted him to hurt.

Carr's eyes widened. He lifted the knife.

When he swung at me, I aimed for his arm. My blow hit his forearm, and I heard bone snap. The knife flew out of his hand and hit the wall. He cried out.

"Take me on," I said. "I'm not a young, defenseless woman."

I landed a hard jab, then a right. I hammered blows into his torso, his body shuddering under the impact.

Bell stepped closer and punched him in the stomach. We hit him together.

"That's for Karina." She punched him again. "That one's for Allie." Bell's next punch had blood flying from Carr's mouth. "That's for the other women you killed." A vicious uppercut to the man's gut. "That's for me."

He doubled over, cradling his midsection.

I glared at him. "Dante, Simon should be here soon. Call him."

"Will do," my brother replied.

Carr stayed bent over, breathing hard. It sounded like he couldn't breathe properly through his nose, and I shot him a grim smile.

"I told you that it ends here," Bell said.

The killer looked up. "You were supposed to die. I imagined it so many times."

"Sick fuck," Colt muttered.

"Your power over me is gone." She looked at me and smiled. "I've learned not to be afraid."

"I can still make you hurt." With his left hand, Carr whipped another knife—a switchblade—from his back pocket. It snicked open and he hurtled forward.

At me.

It all happened so fast. I tensed.

"No!" Bell yelled. She ran forward and hit Carr from the side.

I watched as they hit the flimsy front windows. They crashed through and glass shattered.

Horror filled me as Carr and Bell fell out the window.

"Bell!"

I heard my brothers cursing. I sprinted for the front door. Crossing the porch in two strides, I leaped over the railing.

"Bell!" My heart was in my fucking throat.

"I'm all right." She pushed herself up. She was lying on top of Carr in the overgrown bushes.

I scooped her into my arms, expecting to see her cut up and bleeding. She had a few small cuts on her face, but otherwise she looked okay.

"Angel?"

She cupped my cheek. "I'm all right, Beau. He broke my fall."

"Shit," Dante muttered.

My brothers stood nearby, as always, having my back.

Still holding her tight, I turned to look.

Carr lay on the ground, moving weakly. He covered in shards of glass and bleeding heavily. One large shard was lodged in his neck. He coughed and I saw blood on his lips.

Bell watched him impassively.

That's when I heard the sirens. A moment later, blue and red lights lit up the cabin as several police cars pulled up.

Simon jogged over and saw Carr. "Hell." He turned. "We need the paramedics." Then the detective looked at me and the woman in my arms. "Is Bell okay?"

"I'm okay," she replied.

"She went through the window with Carr. He took the brunt of it." I held her tighter. It could have been a very different outcome.

"I wasn't going to let him stab you," she said.

"I would have dealt with him."

Her gaze narrowed. "You can protect me, but I can't protect you? No way. I wasn't going to let that man hurt you."

"Bell..." I just hugged her tighter and she buried her face in my neck.

"I need to take everyone's statements," Simon said.

I nodded, then moved over to the front steps. I sat down with Bell on my lap.

"You have glass in your cheek."

"I don't feel it." She smiled. "He's done. He can't hurt anyone ever again."

"Yeah, angel. He's done. Because of you. Because you told me about the note he'd left you. Because we made a plan."

I hadn't loved the plan. It had required her to face Carr alone for a few minutes while my brothers and I had gotten into position, and that was a few minutes too long for me.

"We won." She pulled me close and kissed me. "Thank you, Beauden Fury. For helping me, protecting me, and teaching me to stand on my own."

"You were already doing that, you just needed someone at your back."

"I'm glad it's you."

I held her close as the cops and paramedics bustled around. I wished I could have her back always.

But I already knew that the clock was ticking to the moment when she'd leave. She was finally free to live her life as she chose.

36

BELL

I hummed as I washed the shampoo out of my hair. It was late and we were back at Beau's place.

All I'd wanted was to wash Chandler William Carr off me, and out of my life.

Once and for all.

He'd been taken away in an ambulance under police escort, and now, I didn't want to think about him anymore.

I stood under the warm spray. I was alive, and I wasn't hurt. Well, I had a few small cuts, but a smiling, female paramedic had pulled the tiny slivers of glass from my cheek and put some tape on the worst of them.

Shutting off the water, I grabbed a towel and dried off. I wrapped it around me and looked at my reflection in the foggy mirror. For a second, I imagined I saw Allie standing beside me, looking back at me, smiling.

Live, Bell. Live, love, have fun.

I blinked, and all I saw was my own reflection. I smiled.

I love you, Allie.

I went looking for Beau. The bedroom was dark, just the glimmer of the city lights coming through the windows. I saw his silhouette as he looked out the window.

He was tense and silent.

"Beau?"

He didn't turn, but I saw him raise his arm. He was holding a glass. He sipped, and I guessed it was whiskey.

"So much could have gone wrong tonight." His voice was low and gritty.

"But it didn't."

"He could have grabbed you and run before I got there. He could have stabbed you. It's pure luck you didn't get cut up by the window."

I moved closer, realizing just how upset he was.

"I'm fine, Beau. We're all okay." I touched his back.

His big body shuddered. "Every minute of the drive to get to you, I imagined all the things that could go wrong. All the ways you could get hurt."

I leaned into him. "I'm alive. I'm not hurt."

There was a *clunk* as he set the glass down on the bedside table. He turned, his eyes on me like a laser. I felt the intensity of his gaze.

"Prove it."

I met his gaze for a moment, then I dropped the towel.

His growl was low and deep. He lifted me off my feet, and a second later, my back hit the bed.

Then his mouth was on me. Everywhere. His beard scraped over my sensitive skin. He kissed my cheeks, my neck, my collarbones. His mouth moved lower, over my breasts and stomach and thighs.

I was a writhing mass of pleasure. "*Beau*." My voice was breathy, and I was lost in the sensations.

"My angel." He pushed my thighs apart and slid his big palms under my ass. "I need you." Then he lifted me to his mouth.

"Yes. God, *yes*." I wrapped my thighs around his head.

The swipe of his tongue had me crying out. His slow, greedy licks had me grinding against his mouth. He ate me like a man possessed, like he'd never get enough. His lips closed over my clit, and he alternated between teasing licks and hard sucks.

Hot tension coiled inside me, then the pleasure burst.

I came hard, my vision blurring, as I cried out his name.

"Need to fuck you now." He flipped me onto my stomach. "Need to watch you take me."

"Always," I panted. "I'm always ready to take you."

He pushed me to my knees, and I turned my head to press my cheek to the sheets. I felt his fingers glide through my slick folds.

Then I felt something else. He pulled my wrists behind my back, and I felt him tie them with a silky cord.

My belly quivered.

His big body leaned over me. He'd taken his shirt off, and I felt his hot skin against my back. He nipped my ear lobe. "Like that?"

"Yes." I nodded against the covers.

"All mine. You're right here where I can keep you safe."

"Beau, please—"

"Right where I can do whatever I want to you."

He shifted behind me, and I felt his big cock notch between my legs. His palm was on my ass, his fingers kneading my buttock. His cock was hot as he slid home slowly.

I moaned, pushing back against him.

"Don't move."

I froze.

He sank into me all the way, as deep as he could go.

"*There*. Fuck, angel. I love the way you take me."

Then he started to thrust.

I moaned loudly and squirmed. He filled me, demanding and all-consuming. He hit every nerve ending. I felt so stretched, so taken, so claimed.

His big body covered mine, and I felt his gaze on me, unwavering.

"Angel."

"Beau."

As his thrusts got harder, and more possessive, all I could do was hold on and whimper. I clasped my fingers together. Then I felt his hand slide under my belly. His thumb found my clit.

I cried out. His other hand dug into my hip.

"You love when I take you hard," he growled.

"Yes. I love it." *I love you.* "More. I can't get enough."

He growled, then pulled out. I made a sound of complaint.

Then my hands were free, and I was on my back. His

powerful body settled on mine and then he was back inside me.

His thrusts picked up speed.

"Need to see your face. Need to watch when you come." He groaned. "I can feel you tightening on my cock. Bell, nothing feels as good as you."

"Beau, nothing has ever felt this good," I gasped.

On his next hard thrust, I came. I scratched, I screamed, I shuddered. I felt his cock swell, then he made a low, sexy sound and came. I held on as his big body shook.

Both of us were wrecked. He rolled to the side, pulling me close. Our skin was slick with perspiration, our chests rising and falling fast.

"My angel."

I snuggled into his strength. I'd come hard, twice. I was being held by Beau. Carr was gone.

I smiled. I was free.

Tingles of excitement filled me. I was free to do whatever I wanted. To see my mom, finish college, whatever felt right.

And Beau. I knew I wanted him. I knew that we could make something special together.

"Sleep now," he murmured, pressing a kiss to the side of my head.

My eyelids fluttered, exhaustion dragging me under. Yes, tomorrow, we'd talk and plan the future.

37

BEAU

I listened to the familiar sounds of the gym—the slap of gloves, the grunts and chatter, the *clunk* of weights.

It was just like any other day.

But so much had changed.

Bell—sweet, strong, vulnerable Bell—had entered my world and changed it.

Now, she was finally safe.

Simon had called. Carr had lost too much blood, and hadn't survived his injuries. I felt nothing. The man had been a monster, and I wasn't sorry he was dead. Allie, Karina, and his other victims could now rest in peace.

Bell could live in peace.

I'd left her in my bed—rumpled and exhausted. I should be ashamed of how often I'd taken her during the night. I'd been desperate for her.

Each time, she'd welcomed me with hungry eagerness.

She was safe. She was free.

Now, it was time for me to set her free.

Gio appeared, giving me a look. "You okay?"

"Never better." I leaned back in my office chair. "A serial killer is off the streets and Bell is safe."

The older man nodded. "Good. That girl deserves nothing but good." He slapped the doorframe and disappeared back into the gym.

On that, we could agree.

And despite what my brothers thought, I wasn't good for Bell. I was a tattooed former merc who was good with his fists. Who'd fought and clawed his way through life. Who came from people whose DNA shouldn't be shared.

"Hey, Gio." Bell's voice just outside my office.

She sounded light, happy. I heard them talking, and heard her laugh. Under the desk, my hands curled into fists. I looked down at them and saw how nicked and scarred they were.

Bell appeared in the doorway. Her dark hair was loose, and her smile was big. "Good morning."

"Morning," I replied.

"Thanks for letting me sleep in."

"You needed it."

"I know." Her lips twitched. "But the reason I was tired was so worth it."

I forced myself to stay cool. I had to do what was right for Bell, what was best. "Simon called."

I saw her tense a little.

"Carr died in the hospital."

"Oh." Her smile slipped and she clasped her hands together. Then she shook her head. "I suppose I should feel something...but I don't. I hated him, feared him, for so long. Knowing he's gone, well, it just lifts a weight. I feel relief."

"It doesn't make you a bad person to feel that way after everything."

She nodded.

I pulled in a deep breath. "So, when are you leaving for Texas?"

She blinked. "What?"

"You're safe now. Like you said, the burden of Carr isn't weighing you down anymore. You can see your mom. Go back to school. Go home."

She took a step toward the desk. "I've been the happiest I've ever been here, in New Orleans." She straightened. "With you."

I made a scoffing sound. "You're too smart to work in the gym, Bell. And too smart to stay with a guy like me."

She cocked her head. "A guy like you?"

Dammit. She was making this hard. I rose. "Come on, we both know I'm too old for you, too rough, too... You know what I come from, and you deserve to go out there and find the right guy for you. Make the right life for you."

Her face turned pinched. "I thought I'd found the right guy."

Her words were like a kick to my chest.

She strode closer, and slapped her hands on my desk. "I thought I'd found a man who supported me, protected me. One who, in bed, lights me up in ways I've never imagined. A man who holds me tight in his strong arms."

Fuck. I looked at the floor. "It was never going to be forever. I don't do forever."

"Because you don't want it or don't think you deserve it?"

My head jerked up.

"You do, Beau. Your parents might have been bad people, but you aren't. I know you can't believe every foster kid out there with bad parents deserves to cut themselves off from love."

Hell, she made me want to believe. I wanted to grab her and hold her tight.

But I cared enough to do what was best for her.

Fuck, I loved her. I felt a thud in my chest. I loved her so much and wanted everything for her.

"This—" I waved a hand between us "—has run its course, angel. It's time for you to go home."

To my horror, tears formed in her eyes. She looked at me—strong and direct—as the glittering tears spilled down her cheeks.

Fuck, they cut deep.

"All the words about having my back, being a team, doing things together was garbage." A small, painful laugh escaped her. "I was busy falling in love with you, and you've been waiting for a chance to shove me out the door."

Fucking fuck. The breath was knocked out of me.

"I was a coward for running from Carr, from life, for so long. Now, you're the coward, Beauden. You've been running your entire life. You miss all the good stuff when you do that."

"That's not what this is." But it was. She'd hit the target perfectly.

She nodded, and took a step toward the door. "You want me gone, then I'm gone."

Then she turned and ran out of the office.

I stared at the empty doorway for a long time. My heart was still beating, but it hurt. It hurt with every beat.

I hung my head. This was the way it had to be. What was best for Bell?

38

BELL

I raced through the gym, heading for the front door.

"Girly?"

I didn't respond to the worried Gio. I ran out on the sidewalk and sucked in air. But nothing was going to help the pain inside me.

I wrapped my arms around myself, but the hurt was there, trying to fill my chest and choke me.

I'd fallen in love with Beauden, and he...I had no idea how he felt. Back in his office, he'd been so cold, so disconnected. So unlike the man who'd been taking care of me all this time.

More tears welled.

Not knowing what to do, I headed down the sidewalk. My stomach felt sick, my chest was tight. Tears poured down my cheeks. At least I could be outside safely now. Beau had waited until I was safe before he'd booted me out.

Maybe I'd been spinning my own fantasy about him.

Why would he want a young, inexperienced woman like me?

"Bell?"

My head jerked up. Mila stood in front of me.

"Oh, my God, what's wrong?" She grabbed my shoulders. "Dante got home late last night, but he said that you and Beau were okay. And Carr is gone."

I nodded and wiped my hand across my cheek. "I'm fine. It's all over."

"You should be happy, not devastated."

My chest hitched. "Beau just gave me my marching orders. Asked me when I'm headed back to Texas."

Mila's gaze narrowed. "That idiot."

A sob burst from my chest. "He can't help the way he feels. I fell in love with him, but for him—" I threw my arms up. "I have no idea what it was for him."

Mila slid an arm around me. "That man is cross-eyed in love with you. Clearly it has short-circuited his brain."

I was too tired and sad to fight her. She led me down the street and pushed open a door. Blearily, I noted it was an office.

"Hey, there." Macy rose from behind a desk. She was wearing a jaunty yellow skirt and a cute white shirt. When she saw me, her face turned stricken. "What's wrong? I thought we were celebrating that the evil bad guy is finished."

Mila pushed me into a chair. "Beau told her it's over."

Macy put her hands on her hips. "That idiot."

"Can you get her some tea?" Mila asked.

As Macy bustled off to a small kitchenette, Mila

hitched herself up on the desk. "We need to come up with a plan to make that man see reason."

I curled my hands together in my lap. "I appreciate it, Mila, but like I said, I can't make Beau want me—" I swallowed "—or love me."

"Here." Macy pressed a cup of tea into my hands. "And you don't need to make him love you, because the big lug already does."

I sipped the tea, but it was like my tastebuds had taken the day off. I tasted nothing. It was like all the color, sound, and feeling had all been sucked away, leaving the world gray.

"I think he wanted to help me. Like a savior complex. Now that I'm safe, he's ready to move on."

"Bullshit." Macy crossed her arms over her chest. "I saw him with you."

"Me too," Mila said.

My heart kicked, and I wanted to believe them. A fresh wave of tears threatened, and I swiped at them.

There was a sound. I looked up and saw Colt standing in the doorway to what I guessed was his office. He looked unhappy.

"Sorry to interrupt your work," I said.

He sighed. "Beau always seemed the most...sorted of us all. He did a stint in the military, mainly to watch over Reath. Then he went his own way as a mercenary. Worked in some hellish places. He was a good soldier."

I'm a killer, Bell. I swallowed as I remembered him telling me that. Like he expected me to push him away.

"And he's a brilliant boxer," Colt continued. "He's

used all these things to keep himself busy, and he's never truly confronted his demons."

"His parents," I whispered. "He thinks he comes from trash."

Macy made a sound, and Colt closed the distance to her. He ran a hand down her back. "Yeah. He's been trying to outrun them for years."

"They have *nothing* to do with him," I snapped.

Colt nodded. "We all know that, but some insecurities are fueled by old fears and emotions. They aren't always rational."

I'd never heard Colt talk this much before.

"He's the man he's made himself to be," I said. "Everything he is has nothing to do with them. And I don't mean his gym or his achievements, I mean the way he looks out for his family and friends, the kids he trains in his gym. He's the best man I've ever known."

"Then make him see that, Bell. He looks at you and he sees a smart, beautiful, young woman with her life ahead of her." Colt shook his head. "He's doing this because he's decided you need to go and live a beautiful life."

Emotions hit me. They were all threaded with anger and sympathy for that young boy let down by the people who'd birthed him, who were supposed to love and protect him. It rose up inside me like a wave. Standing, I set the teacup on the desk.

"I want a beautiful life. *This* one. The one I've been making with Beau."

Colt's lips twitched. "So take it. You survived a serial killer, so I'm certain you can get my hardheaded brother to see reason." Colt paused. "And see that you're the best thing that ever happened to him." The man curled his arm around Macy.

The blonde leaned into him.

My anger took over. "How dare Beauden decide what's best for me?"

"That's right," Mila said.

"How dare he decide to shove me away because he thinks it's what's right for me? I know what's right for me."

Mila nodded. "Now, what are you going to do about it?"

"I'm going to show Beauden Fury who's boss." I spun and stormed out.

39

BEAU

"You're a freaking idiot."

Gio's words lashed at me as I strode through Hard Burn looking for...anything to do.

I couldn't think straight. I kept seeing Bell's face, her tears.

"Enough, Gio."

"I told you not to hurt her. Now you've broken her heart, and your own. Bloody idiot."

I spun. "It's better this way."

Gio scoffed. "You don't really believe that."

I stepped forward until my face was an inch from his, my fingers forming a fist. My chest heaved.

My old friend looked at my fist, then my face.

"She's free," I said. "To go and do whatever she wants." I wanted that for her. "If you don't think that this fucking tears me apart—" I spun and pressed my hands to the back of my neck.

The pain would dull...eventually. But I knew that missing her would never go away.

"Beau, if you love her, claim her," Gio said. "Be with her. Don't mess it up like I did. I lost the best thing that ever happened to me, and I regret it every day."

I wanted to howl in agony.

The gym's front door opened.

"Beauden Fury."

I whirled.

Bell strode in, her face set, her body vibrating with energy.

Behind her, I spotted Mila, Colt, and Macy.

But I only had eyes for Bell.

She stopped a foot away. The few people who were working out at the gym stopped to look at us.

"I love you," she said loudly.

My insides clenched. "Bell—"

She held up a hand like a drill sergeant. "No, I'm talking. You said your piece before, and it was bullshit." She poked me in the chest. "I decide how I want to live my life. I survived Carr, I decide what I do now, and where I do it, *not* you." She poked me again. "And I want to live here, with you. I want to be with you."

I stared at her, speechless.

"Because I'm in love with you, Beau. I'm in love with the man who stepped in to help me in that diner. Who took care of me, who loved me that night, and who did it again when I turned up here. He held my hand as I found my courage. He gave me strength, support, and love."

She unmanned me.

"And you love me, Beau."

She pressed her palm to my chest, and I knew she'd feel my heart hammering.

"Everything you've done for me has shown me that you're a good man. Even this morning's misguided attempt at whatever the hell it was. Actions speak louder than words. Carr taught me that. He looked the clean-cut nice guy, who was raised by a good family, but under it, he was a monster. Everything he did showed how ugly he was. Every action you take speaks to your character. The blood in your veins doesn't make you who you are."

"Bell—" My voice was low.

She shook her head. "I'm still not done." She pulled in a breath. "I love you. Now, I'm done."

"My turn," I said.

"As long as you aren't going to be a knuckleheaded idiot."

I glanced over at a scowling Gio, who had his arms crossed over his barrel chest. Colt was wearing a faint smile. Mila and Macy were watching me expectantly. My gym goers were all rapt by the impromptu entertainment.

I focused on Bell. Here she was, being brave again. I pulled her into my arms. "I'm still not sure I deserve you, but I do love you, Bell."

Her face changed. The hard lines melted away as her features softened.

"I love you more than I can ever tell you, or show you. And you might all think I'm an idiot, but I wanted to give you a chance to go back to your old life, if that's what you wanted."

"There is no old life. It's my past. I want to live this present life."

"Then you do that with me."

She smiled. "I feel like I should make you grovel some more."

I dropped to my knees, wrapped my arms around her, and pressed my face to her stomach. "I'm sorry, angel. I hated seeing you cry. Forgive me?"

"Beau." She tugged me up. "I forgive you." Then she went up on her toes and pressed her mouth to mine. She leaped up and I caught her. She wrapped her legs around my waist.

She was right where I wanted her.

I nibbled at her lips and lowered my voice. "I couldn't have stayed away." I knew in my heart I would have caved eventually. "You might be pregnant with our baby."

She gasped. Everyone gasped. Clearly my voice hadn't been low enough.

"That's not why I want you to stay with me," she said.

"That's not why I want you to stay with me, either." I nuzzled her cheek. "I want you because you're mine and I love you."

Her eyes glimmered. "Beau."

I kissed her again.

This kiss was deep and forceful. A claiming. One I'd never let be undone.

I was keeping Isabella "Bell" Sanderson. *Forever*.

No one would ever hunt her, hurt her, or scare her again.

Not when I'd be with her, at her side, always.

40

BELL

A month later

The upbeat jazz music from the live band echoed over the bayou.

I laughed as I twirled, my flirty, calf-length white dress spinning around me.

Lights were strung up overhead, twinkling like fireflies, and people were dancing on the platform over the dark water. Mila's inspired cocktails were being served by some of Dante's waitstaff.

It was the perfect wedding.

I spun back into my husband's strong arms. Beau wore a snow-white shirt with a gray vest that matched the color of his eyes. The sleeves of the shirt were rolled up, and that ink that I loved was on full display. He also had a red rose in his pocket that matched the roses I'd had in my small bouquet.

"Love you, Mrs. Fury," he murmured, moving us into a slow dance despite the fast pace of the music.

My belly hitched. *Mrs. Fury*. I really liked hearing that.

"I love you too, Beau. Thank you for today."

"Thank you for saying yes."

He'd asked me to marry him two weeks ago, right in the middle of Hard Burn. He'd dropped down on one knee and held up a box holding a classic, oval-shaped diamond ring in it.

I'd been speechless, unable to talk.

Once the man had let go of his grip on some of those old demons, he went after what he wanted at full speed. And he let nothing get in his way.

I'd eventually been able to babble out a yes, then he'd slipped the ring onto my finger, and kissed me in the middle of the gym, while our friends and clients had clapped.

And that had led to a small, fun wedding on the bayou.

His brothers and their women danced past us. I smiled. Mila winked, just before Dante bent her back over his arm and planted a kiss on her mouth. Colt, Macy, and Daisy were dancing together as a trio. The little girl was in her pink and white flower girl dress. She blew me a kiss.

Kav and London, and Frankie and Reath whirled past us, all of them smiling.

We had other friends and family celebrating with us. Gio was busy hoovering up Cajun food. Beau's friend who owned the land had catered for us.

I spotted my mom by the railing and waved. She waved back, then dabbed at her eyes. She'd been crying ever since I called her to say that Carr was dead and that I was all right. She'd been staying in New Orleans the last two weeks.

As I'd predicted, she loved Beau.

I wasn't pregnant, and after a discussion, I'd started on birth control.

"You're still young, Bell. We have time." Beau had cupped my cheek. *"We'll make pretty babies. When we're both ready."*

Over the last few weeks, I'd seen some subtle changes in my man. I think it had helped that he'd seen how happy I was. He no longer spoke about not deserving me. I think the past was finally loosening its hold on him. I knew becoming a father in the future would help too. He'd be an amazing, overprotective daddy one day.

Beau pulled me closer. I leaned into his chest and breathed him in. "You smell good."

"So do you," he said. "Like mangoes."

I smiled up at him.

"I look forward to you wearing nothing but that perfume on our honeymoon." He sent me a slow smile.

"You still haven't told me where we're going yet."

"I'll give you a hint." He nodded across the platform.

Ro Langston stood at the railing, talking on his cellphone. He looked to be having a rather heated conversation. I watched as he raked a hand through his brown hair. The last I'd heard, his new mountain resort acquisition was giving him a headache. It seemed the locals of Windward, Colorado were not that keen for their resort to be rolled into Langston Hotels. I was sure he'd convince them, eventually. He was a man who liked a challenge.

"That's not a clue, Beau. The man owns a gazillion resorts and hotels."

He nipped my ear. "You'll like it, I promise."

Of course I would. Uninterrupted time with my hot husband. I didn't care where we went.

"Are you sure we can be away from Hard Burn for three weeks?" I asked.

"Yes. Gio will be in charge, and my brothers will look in and help out." He squeezed my ass. "Stop worrying. Your work will still be there when we get back."

I'd taken on a little more of the business side of things, which freed Beau up to train more clients. He had zero complaints. I was currently setting up an online store to sell Beauden Fury approved merchandise and boxing gear. I already had huge interest from the gym's clients. I felt a tingle of excitement. After our honeymoon, I was also going back to college at the University of New Orleans. I couldn't wait to finish my degree.

I tipped my head back. I had everything I wanted. My life was night and day from where it had been a few months ago. I'd gone from having nothing, to having a life I'd never let myself dream about.

I looked up at the stars overhead. One blinked, then another, and I smiled. My thoughts turned to Karina and Allie. I'd attended Karina's funeral, and cried my eyes out against Beau's chest, and then with Karina's mother. The older woman hadn't blamed me for her daughter's death.

My girl had a big heart. I know she was looking over

you when you took down the man who stole her away from us.

I knew Karina and Allie would be happy for me today. I vowed to make every day count, for all of us.

Wish you could have had your own Fury brother, Allie.

"Happy?" Beau asked.

"I blew way past happy ages ago." I cupped his face. "Now, what do I have to do to get a kiss from my husband?"

"Just ask."

"Kiss me, Mr. Fury."

His mouth covered mine as we danced on the bayou, surrounded by everyone we loved.

I hope you enjoyed Beau and Bell's story!

I hope you've loved the Fury Brothers as much as I've loved writing them!

Keep an eye out for my brand-new series, LANGSTON HOTELS, starring Ambrose "Ro" Langston. This is city meets small town, as Ro and his high-powered executive team face off with the locals of the Windward Mountain Resort. Coming later in 2025.

For more action-packed contemporary romance, check out the first book in the **Billionaire Heists**, *Stealing* *from Mr. Rich* (Monroe and Zane's story). **Read on for a preview of the first chapter.**

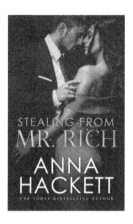

Don't miss out! For updates about new releases, free books, and other fun stuff, sign up for my VIP mailing list and get your *free box set* containing three action-packed romances.

Visit here to get started: www.annahackett.com

Would you like a FREE BOX SET of my books?

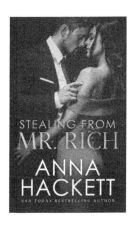

Brother in Trouble

Monroe

The old-fashioned Rosengrens safe was a beauty.

I carefully turned the combination dial, then pressed closer to the safe. The metal was cool under my fingertips. The safe wasn't pretty, but stout and secure. There was something to be said for solid security.

Rosengrens had started making safes in Sweden over a hundred years ago. They were good at it. I listened to the pins, waiting for contact. Newer safes had internals made from lightweight materials to reduce sensory feedback, so I didn't get to use these skills very often.

Some people could play the piano, I could play a safe. The tiny vibration I was waiting for reached my fingertips, followed by the faintest click.

"I've gotcha, old girl." The Rosengrens had quite a few quirks, but my blood sang as I moved the dial again.

I heard a louder click and spun the handle.

The safe door swung open. Inside, I saw stacks of jewelry cases and wads of hundred-dollar bills. *Nice.*

Standing, I dusted my hands off on my jeans. "There you go, Mr. Goldstein."

"You are a doll, Monroe O'Connor. Thank you."

The older man, dressed neatly in pressed chinos and a blue shirt, grinned at me. He had coke-bottle glasses, wispy, white hair, and a wrinkled face.

I smiled at him. Mr. Goldstein was one of my favorite people. "I'll send you my bill."

His grin widened. "I don't know what I'd do without you."

I raised a brow. "You could stop forgetting your safe combination."

The wealthy old man called me every month or so to open his safe. Right now, we were standing in the home office of his expensive Park Avenue penthouse.

It was decorated in what I thought of as "rich, old man." There were heavy drapes, gold-framed artwork, lots of dark wood—including the built-in shelves around the safe—and a huge desk.

"Then I wouldn't get to see your pretty face," he said.

I smiled and patted his shoulder. "I'll see you next month, Mr. Goldstein." The poor man was lonely. His wife had died the year before, and his only son lived in Europe.

"Sure thing, Monroe. I'll have some of those donuts you like."

We headed for the front door and my chest tightened. I understood feeling lonely. "You could do with some new locks on your door. I mean, your building has top-notch security, but you can never be too careful. Pop by the shop if you want to talk locks."

He beamed at me and held the door open. "I might do that."

"Bye, Mr. Goldstein."

I headed down the plush hall to the elevator. Every-thing in the building screamed old money. I felt like an imposter just being in the building. Like I had "daughter of a criminal" stamped on my head.

Pulling out my cell phone, I pulled up my accounting app and entered Mr. Goldstein's callout. Next, I checked my messages.

Still nothing from Maguire.

Frowning, I bit my lip. That made it three days since I'd heard from my little brother. I shot him off a quick text.

"Text me back, Mag," I muttered.

The elevator opened and I stepped in, trying not to worry about Maguire. He was an adult, but I'd practically raised him. Most days it felt like I had a twenty-four-year-old kid.

The elevator slowed and stopped at another floor. An older, well-dressed couple entered. They eyed me and my well-worn jeans like I'd crawled out from under a rock.

I smiled. "Good morning."

Yeah, yeah, I'm not wearing designer duds, and my bank account doesn't have a gazillion zeros. You're so much better than me.

Ignoring them, I scrolled through Instagram. When we finally reached the lobby, the couple shot me another dubious look before they left. I strode out across the marble-lined space and rolled my eyes.

During my teens, I'd cared about what people thought. Everyone had known that my father was Terry O'Connor—expert thief, safecracker, and con man. I'd felt every repulsed look and sly smirk at high school.

Then I'd grown up, cultivated some thicker skin, and learned not to care. *Fuck 'em.* People who looked down on others for things outside their control were assholes.

I wrinkled my nose. Okay, it was easier said than done.

When I walked outside, the street was busy. I smiled, breathing in the scent of New York—car exhaust, burnt meat, and rotting trash. Besides, most people cared more about themselves. They judged you, left you bleeding, then forgot you in the blink of an eye.

I unlocked my bicycle, and pulled on my helmet, then set off down the street. I needed to get to the store. The ride wasn't long, but I spent every second worrying about Mag.

My brother had a knack for finding trouble. I sighed. After a childhood, where both our mothers had taken off, and Da was in and out of jail, Mag was entitled to being a bit messed up. The O'Connors were a long way from the Brady Bunch.

I pulled up in front of my shop in Hell's Kitchen and stopped for a second.

I grinned. *All mine.*

Okay, I didn't own the building, but I owned the store. The sign above the shop said *Lady Locksmith*. The logo was lipstick red—a woman's hand with gorgeous red nails, holding a set of keys.

After I locked up my bike, I strode inside. A chime sounded.

God, I loved the place. It was filled with glossy, warm-wood shelves lined with displays of state-of-the-art locks and safes. A key-cutting machine sat at the back.

A blonde head popped up from behind a long, shiny counter.

"You're back," Sabrina said.

My best friend looked like a doll—small, petite, with a head of golden curls.

We'd met doing our business degrees at college, and had become fast friends. Sabrina had always wanted to be tall and sexy, but had to settle for small and cute. She was my manager, and was getting married in a month.

"Yeah, Mr. Goldstein forgot his safe code again," I said.

Sabrina snorted. "That old coot doesn't forget, he just likes looking at your ass."

"He's harmless. He's nice, and lonely. How's the team doing?"

Sabrina leaned forward, pulling out her tablet. I often wondered if she slept with it. "Liz is out back unpacking stock." Sabrina's nose wrinkled. "McRoberts overcharged us on the Schlage locks again."

"That prick." He was always trying to screw me over. "I'll call him."

"Paola, Kat, and Isabella are all out on jobs."

Excellent. Business was doing well. Lady Locksmith specialized in providing female locksmiths to all the single ladies of New York. They also advised on how to keep them safe—securing locks, doors, and windows.

I had a dream of one day seeing multiple Lady Locksmiths around the city. Hell, around every city. A girl could dream. Growing up, once I understood the damage my father did to other people, all I'd wanted was to be respectable. To earn my own way and add to the world, not take from it.

"Did you get that new article I sent you to post on the blog?" I asked.

Sabrina nodded. "It'll go live shortly, and then I'll post on Insta, as well."

When I had the time, I wrote articles on how women —single *and* married—should secure their homes. My latest was aimed at domestic-violence survivors, and helping them feel safe. I donated my time to Nightingale House, a local shelter that helped women leaving DV situations, and I installed locks for them, free of charge.

"We should start a podcast," Sabrina said.

I wrinkled my nose. "I don't have time to sit around recording stuff." I did my fair share of callouts for jobs, plus at night I had to stay on top of the business-side of the store.

"Fine, fine." Sabrina leaned against the counter and eyed my jeans. "Damn, I hate you for being tall, long, and gorgeous. You're going to look *way* too beautiful as my maid of honor." She waved a hand between us. "You're all tall, sleek, and dark-haired, and I'm...the opposite."

I had some distant Black Irish ancestor to thank for my pale skin and ink-black hair. Growing up, I wanted to be short, blonde, and tanned. I snorted. "Beauty comes in all different forms, Sabrina." I gripped her shoulders. "You are so damn pretty, and your fiancé happens to think you are the most beautiful woman in the world. Andrew is gaga over you."

Sabrina sighed happily. "He does and he is." A pause. "So, do you have a date for my wedding yet?" My bestie's voice turned breezy and casual.

Uh-oh. I froze. All the wedding prep had sent my normally easygoing best friend a bit crazy. And I knew very well not to trust that tone.

I edged toward my office. "Not yet."

Sabrina's blue eyes sparked. "It's only *four* weeks away, Monroe. The maid of honor can't come alone."

"I'll be busy helping you out—"

"Find a date, Monroe."

"I don't want to just pick anyone for your wedding—"

Sabrina stomped her foot. "Find someone, or I'll find someone for you."

I held up my hands. "Okay, okay." I headed for my office. "I'll—" My cell phone rang. *Yes.* "I've got a call. Got to go." I dove through the office door.

"I won't forget," Sabrina yelled. "I'll revoke your best-friend status, if I have to."

I closed the door on my bridezilla bestie and looked at the phone.

Maguire. Finally.

I stabbed the call button. "Where have you been?"

"We have your brother," a robotic voice said.

My blood ran cold. My chest felt like it had filled with concrete.

"If you want to keep him alive, you'll do exactly as I say."

Zane

God, this party was boring.

Zane Roth sipped his wine and glanced around the ballroom at the Mandarin Oriental. The party held the Who's Who of New York society, all dressed up in their glittering best. The ceiling shimmered with a sea of crystal lights, tall flower arrangements dominated the tables, and the wall of windows had a great view of the Manhattan skyline.

Everything was picture perfect...and boring.

If it wasn't for the charity auction, he wouldn't be dressed in his tuxedo and dodging annoying people.

"I'm so sick of these parties," he muttered.

A snort came from beside him.

One of his best friends, Maverick Rivera, sipped his wine. "You were voted New York's sexiest billionaire bachelor. You should be loving this shindig."

Mav had been one of his best friends since college. Like Zane, Maverick hadn't come from wealth. They'd both earned it the old-fashioned way. Zane loved numbers and money, and had made Wall Street his hunting ground. Mav was a geek, despite not looking like a stereotypical one. He'd grown up in a strong, Mexican-American family, and with his brown skin, broad shoulders, and the fact that he worked out a lot, no one would pick him for a tech billionaire.

But under the big body, the man was a computer geek to the bone.

"All the society mamas are giving you lots of speculative looks." Mav gave him a small grin.

"Shut it, Rivera."

"They're all dreaming of marrying their daughters off to billionaire Zane Roth, the finance King of Wall Street."

Zane glared. "You done?"

"Oh, I could go on."

"I seem to recall another article about the billionaire bachelors. All three of us." Zane tipped his glass at his friend. "They'll be coming for you, next."

Mav's smile dissolved, and he shrugged a broad shoulder. "I'll toss Kensington at them. He's pretty."

Liam Kensington was the third member of their trio. Unlike Zane and Mav, Liam had come from money, although he worked hard to avoid his bloodsucking family.

Zane saw a woman in a slinky, blue dress shoot him a welcoming smile.

He looked away.

When he'd made his first billion, he'd welcomed the attention. Especially the female attention. He'd bedded more than his fair share of gorgeous women.

Of late, nothing and no one caught his interest. Women all left him feeling numb.

Work. He thrived on that.

A part of him figured he'd never find a woman who made him feel the same way as his work.

"Speak of the devil," Mav said.

Zane looked up to see Liam Kensington striding toward them. With the lean body of a swimmer, clad in a perfectly tailored tuxedo, he looked every inch the billionaire. His gold hair complemented a face the ladies oohed over.

People tried to get his attention, but the real estate mogul ignored everyone.

He reached Zane and Mav, grabbed Zane's wine, and emptied it in two gulps.

"I hate this party. When can we leave?" Having spent his formative years in London, he had a posh British accent. Another thing the ladies loved. "I have a contract to work on, my fundraiser ball to plan, and things to catch up on after our trip to San Francisco."

The three of them had just returned from a business trip to the West Coast.

"Can't leave until the auction's done," Zane said.

Liam sighed. His handsome face often had him voted the best-looking billionaire bachelor.

"Buy up big," Zane said. "Proceeds go to the Boys and Girls Clubs."

"One of your pet charities," Liam said.

"Yeah." Zane's father had left when he was seven. His mom had worked hard to support them. She was his hero. He liked to give back to charities that supported kids growing up in tough circumstances.

He'd set his mom up in a gorgeous house Upstate that she loved. And he was here for her tonight.

"Don't bid on the Phillips-Morley necklace, though," he added. "It's mine."

The necklace had a huge, rectangular sapphire pendant surrounded by diamonds. It was the real-life necklace said to have inspired the necklace in the movie, *Titanic*. It had been given to a young woman, Kate Florence Phillips, by her lover, Henry Samuel Morley. The two had run away together and booked passage on the Titanic.

Unfortunately for poor Kate, Henry had drowned when the ship had sunk. She'd returned to England with the necklace and a baby in her belly.

Zane's mother had always loved the story and pored over pictures of the necklace. She'd told him the story of the lovers, over and over.

"It was a gift from a man to a woman he loved. She was a shop girl, and he owned the store, but they fell in love, even though society frowned on their love." She sighed. "That's true love, Zane. Devotion, loyalty, through the good times and the bad."

Everything Carol Roth had never known.

Of course, it turned out old Henry was much older than his lover, and already married. But Zane didn't want to ruin the fairy tale for his mom.

Now, the Phillips-Morley necklace had turned up, and was being offered at auction. And Zane was going to get it for his mom. It was her birthday in a few months.

"Hey, is your fancy, new safe ready yet?" Zane asked Mav.

His friend nodded. "You're getting one of the first ones. I can have my team install it this week."

"Perfect." Mav's new Riv3000 was the latest in high-tech safes and said to be unbreakable. "I'll keep the necklace in it until my mom's birthday."

Someone called out Liam's name. With a sigh, their friend forced a smile. "Can't dodge this one. Simpson's an investor in my Brooklyn project. I'll be back."

"Need a refill?" Zane asked Mav.

"Sure."

Zane headed for the bar. He'd almost reached it when a manicured hand snagged his arm.

"Zane."

He looked down at the woman and barely swallowed his groan. "Allegra. You look lovely this evening."

She did. Allegra Montgomery's shimmery, silver dress

hugged her slender figure, and her cloud of mahogany brown hair accented her beautiful face. As the only daughter of a wealthy New York family—her father was from *the* Montgomery family and her mother was a former Miss America—Allegra was well-bred and well-educated but also, as he'd discovered, spoiled and liked getting her way.

Her dark eyes bored into him. "I'm sorry things ended badly for us the other month. I was..." Her voice lowered, and she stroked his forearm. "I miss you. I was hoping we could catch up again."

Zane arched a brow. They'd dated for a few weeks, shared a few dinners, and some decent sex. But Allegra liked being the center of attention, complained that he worked too much, and had constantly hounded him to take her on vacation. Preferably on a private jet to Tahiti or the Maldives.

When she'd asked him if it would be too much for him to give her a credit card of her own, for monthly expenses, Zane had exited stage left.

"I don't think so, Allegra. We aren't...compatible."

Her full lips turned into a pout. "I thought we were *very* compatible."

He cleared his throat. "I heard you moved on. With Chip Huffington."

Allegra waved a hand. "Oh, that's nothing serious."

And Chip was only a millionaire. Allegra would see that as a step down. In fact, Zane felt like every time she looked at him, he could almost see little dollar signs in her eyes.

He dredged up a smile. "I wish you all the best, Allegra. Good evening." He sidestepped her and made a beeline for the bar.

"What can I get you?" the bartender asked.

Wine wasn't going to cut it. It would probably be frowned on to ask for an entire bottle of Scotch. "Two glasses of Scotch, please. On the rocks. Do you have Macallan?"

"No, sorry, sir. Will Glenfiddich do?"

"Sure."

"Ladies and gentlemen," a voice said over the loud-speaker. The lights lowered. "I hope you're ready to spend big for a wonderful cause."

Carrying the drinks, Zane hurried back to Mav and Liam. He handed Mav a glass.

"Let's do this," Mav grumbled. "And next time, I'll make a generous online donation so I don't have to come to the party."

"Drinks at my place after I get the necklace," Zane said. "I have a very good bottle of Macallan."

Mav stilled. "How good?"

"Macallan 25. Single malt."

"I'm there," Liam said.

Mav lifted his chin.

Ahead, Zane watched the evening's host lift a black cloth off a pedestal. He stared at the necklace, the sapphire glittering under the lights.

There it was.

The sapphire was a deep, rich blue. Just like all the photos his mother had shown him.

"Get that damn necklace, Roth, and let's get out of here," Mav said.

Zane nodded. He'd get the necklace for the one woman in his life who rarely asked for anything, then escape the rest of the bloodsuckers and hang with his friends.

Billionaire Heists

Stealing from Mr. Rich
Blackmailing Mr. Bossman
Hacking Mr. CEO

PREVIEW: NORCROSS SECURITY

Want more action-packed romance? Then check out the men of **Norcross Security**.

The only man who can keep her safe is her boss' gorgeous brother.

Museum curator Haven McKinney has sworn off men. All of them. Totally. She's recently escaped a bad ex and started a new life for herself in San Francisco. She *loves* her job at the Hutton Museum, likes her new boss, and has made best friends with his feisty sister. Haven's also desperately trying *not* to notice their brother: hotshot investigator Rhys Norcross. And she's *really* trying not to notice his muscular body, sexy tattoos, and charming smile.

Nope, Rhys is off limits. But then Haven finds herself in the middle of a deadly situation...

Investigator Rhys Norcross is good at finding his targets. After leaving an elite Ghost Ops military team, the former Delta Force soldier thrives on his job at his brother's security firm, Norcross Security. He's had his eye on smart, sexy Haven for a while, but the pretty curator with her eyes full of secrets is proving far harder to chase down than he anticipated.

Luckily, Rhys never, ever gives up.

When thieves target the museum and steal a multi-million-dollar painting in a daring theft, Haven finds herself in trouble, and dangers from her past rising. Rhys vows to do whatever it takes to keep her safe, and Haven finds herself risking the one thing she was trying so hard to protect—her heart.

Norcross Security

The Investigator
The Troubleshooter
The Specialist
The Bodyguard
The Hacker

The Powerbroker
The Detective
The Medic
The Protector
Also Available as Audiobooks!

ALSO BY ANNA HACKETT

Fury Brothers

Fury

Keep

Burn

Take

Also Available as Audiobooks!

Unbroken Heroes

The Hero She Needs

The Hero She Wants

The Hero She Craves

Also Available as Audiobooks!

Sentinel Security

Wolf

Hades

Striker

Steel

Excalibur

Hex

Stone

Also Available as Audiobooks!

Norcross Security

The Investigator

The Troubleshooter

The Specialist

The Bodyguard

The Hacker

The Powerbroker

The Detective

The Medic

The Protector

Mr. & Mrs. Norcross

Also Available as Audiobooks!

Billionaire Heists

Stealing from Mr. Rich

Blackmailing Mr. Bossman

Hacking Mr. CEO

Also Available as Audiobooks!

Team 52

Mission: Her Protection

Mission: Her Rescue

Mission: Her Security

Mission: Her Defense

Mission: Her Safety

Mission: Her Freedom

Mission: Her Shield

Mission: Her Justice

Also Available as Audiobooks!

Treasure Hunter Security

Undiscovered

Uncharted

Unexplored

Unfathomed

Untraveled

Unmapped

Unidentified

Undetected

Also Available as Audiobooks!

Oronis Knights

Knightmaster

Knighthunter

Galactic Kings

Overlord

Emperor

Captain of the Guard

Conqueror

Also Available as Audiobooks!

Eon Warriors

Edge of Eon

Touch of Eon

Heart of Eon

Kiss of Eon

Mark of Eon

Claim of Eon

Storm of Eon

Soul of Eon

King of Eon

Also Available as Audiobooks!

Galactic Gladiators: House of Rone

Sentinel

Defender

Centurion

Paladin

Guard

Weapons Master

Also Available as Audiobooks!

Galactic Gladiators

Gladiator

Warrior

Hero

Protector

Champion

Barbarian

Beast

Rogue

Guardian

Cyborg

Imperator

Hunter

Also Available as Audiobooks!

Hell Squad

Marcus

Cruz

Gabe

Reed

Roth

Noah

Shaw

Holmes

Niko

Finn

Devlin

Theron

Hemi

Ash

Levi

Manu

Griff

Dom

Survivors

Tane

Also Available as Audiobooks!

The Anomaly Series

Time Thief

Mind Raider

Soul Stealer

Salvation

Anomaly Series Box Set

The Phoenix Adventures

Among Galactic Ruins

At Star's End

In the Devil's Nebula

On a Rogue Planet

Beneath a Trojan Moon

Beyond Galaxy's Edge

On a Cyborg Planet

Return to Dark Earth

On a Barbarian World

Lost in Barbarian Space

Through Uncharted Space

Crashed on an Ice World

Perma Series

Winter Fusion

A Galactic Holiday

Warriors of the Wind

Tempest

Storm & Seduction

Fury & Darkness

Standalone Titles

Savage Dragon

Hunter's Surrender

One Night with the Wolf

For more information visit www.annahackett.com

ABOUT THE AUTHOR

I'm a USA Today bestselling romance author who's passionate about ***fast-paced,*** ***emotion-filled*** contemporary romantic suspense and science fiction romance. I love writing about people overcoming unbeatable odds and achieving seemingly impossible goals. I like to believe it's possible for all of us to do the same.

I live in Australia with my own personal hero and two very busy, always-on-the-move sons.

For release dates, behind-the-scenes info, free books, and other fun stuff, sign up for the latest news here:

Website: www.annahackett.com

Made in United States
North Haven, CT
22 October 2024

59343744R00168